A COUP IN MANILA

Chapter One

"This place is an armpit." Josh Steinberg slouched restlessly on a hardback chair in Gimpo International Airport, Seoul, South Korea. He was on a two-hour layover waiting to connect onward to Manila, his final destination. His journey had started seventeen hours ago at JFK, New York. Four hours to Los Angeles, followed by a one-hour layover, and then a twelve-hour flight from LAX to this hellhole. He was tired, jet-lagged, and hungover. His stomach churned at the thought of having to endure yet another four hours in coach before reaching his final destination.

This was his first trip to Asia. Josh was five years graduated from M.I.T. with a degree in computer science, and he was beginning a six-month overseas posting with his U.S.-based employer, Emerald Systems, Inc. He had been jazzed when the opportunity first presented itself. He was single, currently unattached, and keen for some adventure. Born and raised in Boston, Josh had been to Canada several times, gone down to Cancun exactly once for spring break, and spent the summer after his graduation backpacking in Europe with some buddies before taking up employment with Emerald Systems. Right now, he was pining for the view of the St. Charles River from his one-bedroom apartment in Beacon Hill.

They would be taking the same Boeing 747 that had just flown the Pacific, but there would be a crew change. It had been a rocky enough landing into high winds and driving rain. The layover was extended for thirty minutes due to the weather.

What struck Josh most forcibly about his first experience of Asia was how many people smoked. The air travellers in the terminal were lighting up all over the place. The second-hand smoke caused his eyes to sting, adding to his misery. After what seemed an eternity, they reboarded the plane, and he listened once again to the flight attendants going through their safety demonstration. The takeoff was harrowing. The great four-engine plane was buffeted this way and that as it laboured to gain altitude.

Josh wondered about the competence of the new local crew as he was thrown about violently in his seat. No reassuring announcements came from the flight deck, just the illumination of the fasten seatbelt sign. After about twenty nerve-wracking minutes, the plane levelled off and the turbulence eased.

Josh breathed a sigh of relief and tried to make himself comfortable in his cramped window seat. For the Los Angeles to Seoul leg, the middle seat beside him had been empty, but it was now occupied by a middle-aged Indian woman in a sari who insisted on sitting cross-legged with one of her knees digging into his side.

The four hours were interminable. All he wanted to do was get off the bloody plane.

At last, the lights of Manila came into view. He was relieved to hear that the weather for landing was fair, the temperature 85 degrees Fahrenheit, with a light breeze and 75 per cent humidity.

Customs and immigration were perfunctory, although the form he had to fill out seemed unnecessarily complicated. One glance at his U.S. passport was all that was required before the visa page was stamped and he was waved through by a smiling agent.

The arrivals hall was manic. A noisy, seething sea of humanity confronted Josh. Pushing his luggage on his cart, he looked around anxiously for his driver. He was to spend a couple of nights at the Peninsula Hotel before being assigned an apartment and his HR representative back in the States had warned him that for his own safety, he should only travel in a limousine provided by the hotel.

At last, he saw his name and company on a placard being held up by a limo driver in a dark suit, tie, and cap. Even in the terminal building, his t-shirt was sticking to him and as soon as he walked outside, the humidity felt like hitting a wall.

"Welcome to Manila, Mr Steinberg. Is this your first time?"

His driver wanted to strike up a conversation, but Josh was feeling tired and irritable, and kept his answers monosyllabic. His mood improved as he stretched out in the back of the air-conditioned limo and took a sip from one of its refrigerated bottles of water.

"How far is it to the hotel?" Josh asked.

"About five miles."

"How long to get there?"

"Traffic is not too bad, sir. About an hour."

"An hour!" Josh exclaimed. "At ten at night?"

"Sorry sir, there's a festival."

Josh was going to learn that the Filipinos did not like to lose face. There was always an excuse for why things were not working. However, they might complain about things among themselves, they would never badmouth their country or how it operated to foreigners. For now, Josh just muttered, "For Chrissake."

The journey started uneventfully, with some glimpses of the countryside as they left the perimeter of the airport. Soon, however, they drove along an increasingly crowded two-lane highway, if it could be called that, with a seemingly endless line of tin shacks on either side.

Even though it was late at night, there were people everywhere. Children squatted in front of the slum dwellings or played on the side of the street. There were motorbikes and bicycles, beaten-up trucks, and colourful jeepneys clogging up the road in either direction. Josh had read up on Manila before embarking on his assignment. It was one of the most densely populated cities on earth, with eight million living in the greater metropolitan area and three million of those living in shantytowns. Still, nothing had prepared him for this mass of humanity living in the most squalid conditions he had ever seen in his life. He now understood why the five-mile trip was going to take an hour. The limo driver inched along, weaving as best he could to avoid the pedestrians and motley traffic.

"I need to take a leak," Josh said, cursing himself for not going before leaving the airport. He had imagined he could afford to wait until he reached the comfort and privacy of his hotel room, but he had not taken into account what was now going to be a protracted limo ride.

"I'm sorry, sir?" His driver clearly did not understand the colloquialism.

"I need to go to the bathroom, man," Josh snapped.

"I will stop as soon as it is possible, sir."

The answer infuriated Josh, who felt the pressure in his bladder acutely.

What is the clown waiting for? he thought as the limo continued to crawl along. On reflection, though, he could see that just going behind a wall somewhere would not be an option. There would be too many people, particularly children, and unzipping his fly in public wouldn't be smart. After what seemed forever, the driver pulled into a side street and came round to open the limo door.

"You should be able to use the restroom of this bar, sir. I will wait for you."

Josh looked disbelievingly at the tin shack with the half-lit San Miguel sign his driver indicated. The foetid smell of garbage that hit him when his door opened made him want to retch and a small group of curious children was already gathering. *I'm going to have to chance it,* he thought. *That or risk pissing myself.*

The bar was long and narrow, with room for only the counter and a few stools. Josh asked the wizened Filipino barkeep for a Coke and inquired about the bathroom. It was literally a hole in the ground out back. There was an overwhelming smell of raw sewage coming from the cesspit. He held his breath as he relieved himself and caught out of the corner of his eye a rat scurrying to ground not a foot away. *How can people live like this?* he thought as he gratefully clambered back into the limo.

Just as Josh thought they were finally entering the city proper, they encountered a massive traffic jam at an intersection. The sound of horns was deafening.

"So sorry, sir. It's a power outage. The traffic lights are not working." No one would give way. Traffic was hopelessly snarled.

Fucking great. A crappy end to a crappy day.

After about thirty minutes, three uniformed police appeared on the scene and began directing traffic, clearing up the snarl. Some two hours after leaving the airport, the limousine finally pulled up to the entrance of the Peninsula Hotel, flanked by its iconic Chinese lion statues.

Even exhausted as he was, Josh was stunned by the grandeur of the hotel lobby. A sweeping neoclassical staircase led up to the mezzanine, where an orchestra entertained guests as they sat around sipping cocktails. White-uniformed bellboys with jaunty caps held

6

the doors to the entrance and beautiful young Filipinas in elegant form-hugging skirt suits stood behind the registration counter with welcoming smiles. Checking in was smooth and gracious.

"You have a message, Mr Steinberg." The girl handed him an envelope.

A little surprised, Josh opened it and read: *Welcome to Manila! Will meet you in the lobby for breakfast at 7.00 a.m. and take you over to the office after.* He had to squint to make out the scrawled signature—Lou Holt.

"Ramon can take you to your room, Mr Steinberg. It's on the seventh floor. A bellboy will deliver your bags shortly."

Josh frowned. Once he got to the room, he just wanted to collapse. He did not particularly want to wait around until his bags were delivered before being able to go to sleep.

"Actually, I think I'll have a beer before I turn in. Can the bags just be left in the room?"

"Of course, sir!"

The receptionist was all accommodating charm. Ramon, who had been hovering, looked disappointed, obviously hoping for a decent tip. Josh could give a flying fuck about Ramon.

He trudged over to a leather chair in the atrium and sat down. Almost instantly, a young Filipina in a colourful sari came to take his order. He selected the local brew, San Miguel. It arrived in a frosted glass, and he sipped it appreciatively.

I'm going into sensory overload.

Josh had known next to nothing about the Philippines before embarking on this trip. High school history had covered the Second World War, and from that Josh had registered the Japanese victory at Corregidor, MacArthur's forced evacuation, and subsequent triumphant and well-photographed return. He had learned, in his brief stint of research before his departure, that the country had undergone a population boom. At the start of the war in 1941, the population stood at 17 million; now there were 60 million Filipinos. It was a *very* catholic country. It was also an oligarchy. About 40 families controlled 90 per cent of its wealth, and over half the population lived in squalor. These were simply sanitised facts when he had read them a week ago, but the last few hours had brought them viscerally to life. He could not get his head around the opulence of the scene before him after the abject destitution he had observed on the ride in. He felt as if he had been gut punched.

At a lot of tables, Filipinos were tucking into what looked like ice cream sundaes on steroids. He asked a passing waitress what they were.

"They are halo halo, sir. A favourite dessert in the Philippines. Would you like to try one?"

Josh suppressed a shudder. "No thanks. I'll just pay my bill."

By the time he got to his room, his bags had already been delivered. It was spacious with a giant, king-size bed, a well-stocked minibar, and a cavernous marble bathroom with separate walk-in shower and deep-soak bathtub. Josh stripped down to his boxers, climbed into bed, and passed out.

Chapter Two

Seated at a table tucked discreetly in an alcove beneath the ornate staircase of the Peninsula Hotel, nineteen-year-old Angel Torres and her companion, the much older Philip Wentworth, had a nice view of the registration desk.

Philip liked to observe and comment on almost every guest checking in, a game that helped bolster his already firm sense of superiority. He was English, in his early forties, and wore a Saville Row, worsted wool, three-piece suit with a silk tie and gold cufflinks, despite the tropical climate. He would've fit right in at the library of the Reform Club—of which he was a member—but here the outfit made him stick out like a sore thumb.

"Another American fresh off the plane," Wentworth said, gesturing in the direction of the front desk with his whiskey glass, the Cutty Sark 33-year-old blended Scotch threatening to spill out with every jerk of his hand.

Angel sipped a white wine spritzer, turning her head dutifully in the direction her escort indicated, her eyes running appreciatively over the lean physique of the young man, careful not to show too much interest so as not to arouse jealousy in her pallid, out-ofcondition patron. He was short for an American, five foot eight or so, with short-cropped, curly black hair.

"Jeans, t-shirt, baseball cap on backward, know-it-all attitude." Wentworth was loud enough to draw the eyes of other guests. "You can spot them a mile off."

"I'm sure you're right, Philip," Angel said with a smile. "You have a gift for observing people."

Her flattery was practised and fluid, an art perfected early in her line of work. She made her living by stroking the egos of middle-aged businessmen.

Wentworth grunted with satisfaction and scanned the lobby for other guests to demean, lighting on a couple of Japanese men in suits conversing quietly at a table near the hotel entrance. "There's a couple of representatives of the Yellow Peril brigade. It's amazing to me how your country can be so hospitable to the Japanese, given what they did to you in World War II. I suppose that since the place has been colonised for most of the past four hundred years, the mentality of subjugation is pretty much ingrained." He was oblivious to how patronising and deeply insulting the observation was.

Angel regarded him impassively. "You mentioned you wanted to go to a concert this evening, Philip. Doesn't it start at eight? It's seven-twenty now."

"I know the time, Angel." Wentworth struck the table with the palm of his hand in annoyance. "It will only take us twenty minutes to get to the Cultural Centre. My driver is waiting."

Still, the intervention served its purpose. Lumbering to his feet, he made for the hotel entrance, not bothering to wait for her.

As suspected, they arrived at the Cultural Centre with no time to spare. They were going to a concert given by the Philippine Symphony Orchestra. Patrons streamed in, and they were far from the last to arrive.

Angel was relieved not to have to linger in the foyer, grateful she wouldn't be subjected to the disdainful looks of the married women who knew what she was. She had a thick skin, but the side-glances of those women never failed to remind her that to them she was nothing more than a whore, a sexual plaything for transient foreign businessmen. It was a role she had to play, a job she had to do, like tens of thousands of others from the provinces, where there were large families with little food and no money. In this deeply Catholic country, no one asked awkward questions when she regularly sent pesos home to help her impoverished parents and six younger siblings. The accepted fiction was that she had a good waitressing job in Manila, as if the pay and tips from such a job would be enough to sustain her in the city, never mind having money left over to send back home.

Wentworth had booked an entire box. Another way to show his superiority. "This means we don't have to mingle with the plebes," he said as they took their seats. "Dirt cheap compared to the Festival Hall on the South Bank, but then this crowd is nowhere near the LSO standard. At least they're a sight better than some of the regional UK orchestras I've had to endure, I'll say that for them."

Wentworth was unimpressed with the first arrangement, a work commissioned specifically for the orchestra, billed as a celebration of the Philippine ethnic musical tradition. Angel found it to be strangely evocative of her home village. It reminded her of the music played at family celebrations when she was a child, but her companion couldn't hide his disappointment.

Halfway through the piece, he turned to her. "I didn't pay all this money to see a novelty act." His voice carried to several of the other patrons, and he made an ostentatious show of examining his programme for the rest of the piece.

The second item was Rachmaninoff's second piano concerto with a young Australian soloist. Wentworth grunted with satisfaction as the lyrical strains of the first movement wafted through the recital hall. Halfway through the slow and wistful second movement, he was asleep, snoring softly. He woke with a start to the opening of the third movement, and it took him a few moments to orient himself.

"We'll leave at the interval, I think. That's enough culture for one day. I fancy a nightcap at the bar before we head back."

The bar he referred to was the Dragon Club on Burgos Street in the red-light district. It was where they'd met. She'd been working there a year and was one of a stable of "hostesses" maintained by the proprietor. Her job was to entertain the bored expat businessmen who frequented establishments all along the street.

There was a protocol for how things worked. A patron came in, sat at the bar or a table, and ordered a drink. The mama-san in charge of the girls would signal to one of them to strike up a conversation to see if the guy would stand her a round. If he did not, she would be discreetly waved away and a new girl presented. Once the target agreed, the chosen girl became his companion for the night. As long as he bought her drinks at reasonable intervals, he would not be bothered by anyone else and could relax. If he didn't go with the flow, he would be pestered incessantly until he packed up and left.

The girls were skilled at managing their clients. The men were by turns horny or homesick, aroused or bored. Each mood swing was catered to. Alcohol flowed freely and a kitchen in the back churned out burgers, chips, and fried calamari.

There was a dartboard and a couple of pool tables. Patrons and their girl companions could play games of Jenga or liar's dice. Occasionally, a group of players would be formed with the stakes of the loser having to remove items of clothing. The girls used it as a form of striptease, losing the early rounds on purpose but then turning the tables when things were looking that they might get out of hand. There was a lot of sexual banter, and the men might take some liberties, but the mama-san made sure things didn't get too carnal.

At some point during the night, a guy might decide he wanted to take "his" girl back to his hotel room. If she consented, they would agree to a price. Before he left, though, he would have to pay the bar fine for her. This was a fee charged by the proprietor for the loss of the girl's services for the rest of the evening. While he settled the fine, the girl would disappear out back, change out of her skimpy outfit, and return in a demure frock, ready to be escorted away.

For the girls, it was a precarious, sordid, and risky livelihood. You could refuse to go with a man you didn't really trust. Saying it was your time of the month was a convenient excuse. The bar owners wanted their fines, however, and if you refused too often, there were plenty of other impoverished and desperate girls ready to take your place.

Angel worried constantly about her health and contracting an STD. She showered before intercourse and immediately after, insisting the man wore a condom. She always had a supply handy. Even so, sometimes her client would be too drunk to fit it properly and it would slip off. On a couple of occasions, the condoms broke.

That was why clients like Wentworth were so attractive. He would pay the bar fine for her for the entire period he was in town. It meant she only had to service him. On several nights, he would take her to bed and pass out before he could do anything. He was racist and a pompous bore, but he wasn't violent and was quite generous with his tips.

When they arrived at the Dragon Club, a fellow customer greeted Phillip. "Hey there, Wentworth! How are things going in that fog-bound, rain-swept, armpit of a country you call home?"

Wentworth snorted in derision. "Better for the fact you're nowhere near the place, Metcalfe, you Aussie prick!"

Wentworth's heckler was Todd Metcalfe, a big buff Australian in khaki shorts and an open-collar shirt two sizes too small for him. The buttons at his corpulent midriff looked as if they were about to pop any second. He sat at a table with one of the bar girls and laughed, unfazed by the insult.

"You're just still sour because we wiped the floor with you in the Ashes! What was the score again, three tests to one? No, I got that wrong! Four bloody nothing! What are you having to drink?"

Wentworth plonked himself in the remaining empty chair at the table, leaving Angel to find one for herself. "Scotch, neat, no ice. I'm not planning to get dysentery from this lot's crappy water supply."

Angel did not bother to react to the jibe. The water supply in Manila was perfectly safe, Wentworth just took pleasure in belittling everything about her country. Todd Metcalfe was the only male companion Philip seemed to have any time for. He did not like the company of other men. She suspected that he felt comfortable with Metcalfe because he could patronise him for being Australian. What the two men did have in common was a passion for cricket, a game which made no sense to Angel, and their blatantly racist attitudes.

"Don't get me wrong, Metcalfe. I like Maggie Thatcher, voted for her and the Tories the past three elections, but she's stubborn as a mule." Wentworth scowled as he held his whiskey glass up to the light and examined the colour. "This poll tax she keeps pushing is hugely unpopular. The great unwashed will have none of it, and the Labour Party is making hay. She's got used to having things all her own way and lost the plot. Happens to women if you give them their head, I suppose."

Todd Metcalfe scratched his crotch, unconcerned with the presence of their female companions. "At least she's done a good job of keeping the Commonwealth coloureds out. Not like the Labour party dickheads we've got in. Look at what that asswipe premier of ours Hawke did, letting 40,000 chinks stay in the country just because the commies mowed down their own people in Tiananmen Square. It wasn't our tanks that ran them over for Chrissake!"

The two men chatted desultorily on, the conversation alternating between politics and a postmortem of the Ashes series. After about an hour, Metcalfe had had enough. He knocked back the remaining whiskey in his glass, slammed it down on the table, and hauled himself to his feet.

"I'm out of here. See you, sunshine!"

"Yeah, see you, Metcalfe."

Wentworth's voice was slurred now. His attention had already drifted as his gaze flitted across the other bar patrons. No one there seemed to interest him. He scowled, and without looking at her, told Angel to call for the bill.

He really is an ill-mannered pig, she thought bitterly, though she kept her expression neutral as she fulfilled his request and followed him to the car.

Wentworth dozed on the way back to the hotel, slumped against his companion. It was a short ride at that hour of the night. When they got to the room, he stripped down to his Y fronts and clambered into bed, leaving his clothes piled on a chair. He'd arranged with the hotel concierge to have his suit pressed and shirt freshly laundered after each day. Socks and underwear would get sent to housekeeping at the end of each week.

Wentworth ran his tongue over his lower lip lewdly as he watched Angel undress.

"I'm just going to take a quick shower before coming to bed, Philip." She gave him a practised smile.

"Be sure you're quick about it," he growled.

As the warm water caressed her skin, Angel reflected sombrely on where her life choices had taken her. Her options had been few. In a Catholic country where contraception was frowned upon and abortion was illegal, families were invariably large and, in her case, there were just too many mouths for her parents to feed. She counted herself lucky that she had managed to avoid getting pregnant before she left her village, either by one of the idle young men, or worse, a predatory older relative. Many of her friends had found themselves in that situation.

Two of her female cousins had gone to Hong Kong as domestics for wealthy Chinese families. They had followed their mother, her aunt Asuncion, who had not been home in fifteen years. They worked six days a week, often eighteen hours a day, and lived for Sundays, their statutory day off. They, along with thousands of other Filipinas, would gather on the sidewalks of the downtown business district, sitting on flattened cardboard boxes, and picnic with their fellow domestics, sharing their favourite dishes from home and catching up with the latest news and gossip. The prospect of such a life had been repugnant to Angel, and so she had chosen to take her chances in Manila. As she dried herself, she wondered if she was really any better off.

Her time in the shower was by design, hoping she might stay in long enough for Philip to succumb to the evening's drink. When she returned to the bedroom, it was as she had hoped. The alcohol had proved too much for Wentworth and he was sleeping soundly, flat on his back, his flabby body heaving rhythmically with each exhalation. Angel slipped in beside him, turned her back, and, clinging to the edge of the bed, willed herself to sleep.

At around six a.m. she was woken by Wentworth shaking her roughly by the shoulder.

"You need to get out of here. I have a breakfast meeting in an hour. Meet me in the lobby tonight around seven." He rolled out of bed, went to his trousers strewn on the chair, and pulled five 1,000-peso notes out of his wallet. He tossed them on the pillow beside her head. "Not sure I got my money's worth out of you last night. Too much whiskey."

Angel gathered up the notes as Philip headed for the bathroom. She dressed quickly and left. The doorman gave her a knowing look as she exited the Peninsula's lobby and caught a jeepney headed in the direction of Burgos Street.

Wentworth was not a particularly demanding client, sexually. He was at his most active when he first got to town, but after a couple of days his lust slaked, and she mainly had to put up with clumsy drunken embraces. At least he was never violent towards her, for which she was grateful. One man had beaten her badly when she first started working in the bar. It left her traumatised and frightened, and she had needed a week to get presentable enough to go back to work, even with heavy makeup. Later, she would go to the post office and mail half the money he had given her home to her parents. It would feed the family for a month.

Philip Wentworth was generous. She'd give him that. Though she wished she could like him a little. It would make the time she spent in his company more tolerable. She had other clients who were more agreeable, and back when she was naïve, had even developed feelings for a few, but whatever claims they made, the men only wanted her body, and once they got back on their airplanes home, forgot all about her until the next time.

Angel lived in a room above the bar, which she shared with six other girls. It was cramped and there was only one bathroom, but at least she was safe. The owner bribed the local police to leave them alone, so she was not subject to being sexually harassed or shaken down for money, which would be the case if she tried to live somewhere on her own.

When she got back, she found two of her roommates sleeping. Angel felt no need to join them, having slept sufficiently while with Wentworth. She occupied herself for an hour, doing some much-needed laundry. Then, dressed in a sober frock and with a black lace mantilla in her purse, she left the bar and began walking toward the centre of Makati.

People were already taking their seats in the pews of the greenbelt chapel, located in the heart of the business district. It was a spiritual oasis, open on three sides, nestled in a green space surrounded by modern office buildings. The outer perimeter was ringed by trees that formed a soft buffer from the busy metropolis it served.

The majority of the Filipinas, like Angel, were wearing mantillas. It was only female Western tourists who were not. Angel sat quietly, tolling her rosary beads, and allowed the peace and tranquillity of the place to envelop her. She prayed for her family, her friends, and lastly for herself. She prayed for forgiveness and understanding of the life she led and the choices she had made.

Mass began, and she drew strength from participating in the communal ritual with others, some of whose circumstances were a mirror of her own. Here, she did not feel like an outcast or a pariah. Here she was just a penitent believer like everyone else. When the mass was over, she lingered for a while, chatting with a couple of her friends. Then she made her way directly to the post office and mailed home the letter she had written to her mother, enclosing with it her monthly remittance to the family.

Chapter Three

Lieutenant Bongo Cruz glanced idly at the clock on the wall in front of him. Only three minutes had passed since the last time he looked. In just over an hour, his shift as a supply clerk at Fort Bonifacio would finish, but since he'd finished everything he could for the day, he had no idea how to pass the remaining time. Certainly not by checking the clock every few minutes. This was an unwelcome change from the frantic pace of the past two weeks. There'd been plenty of tasks to keep him busy, with a rotation of infantry divisions and their associated combat support units from Manila to Mindanao to prosecute the fight against the communist insurgency. Now, everyone was where they should be and it would be a while before paperwork started piling up again as requisitions came in to refurbish and resupply the divisions that had just been relieved.

He could've easily kept busy by getting ahead on the future orders that would soon begin pouring in. The list of suppliers had to be constantly updated and lead times for goods and services were always in flux, so it would be a good idea to get started. But head starts weren't really his thing. There was no reward for being an over-achiever, just a bunch of hard work for nothing. He preferred a more laid-back approach to work and life. Sure, it had caused more problems than not in his personal relationships, but that didn't matter much. He was twenty-six, with eight years in the military under his belt, and he didn't need some woman holding him back.

Bongo had enlisted straight out of high school. As a member of the Scout Rangers Regiment, he was deployed to Mindanao to fight the Moro Islamists after basic training. Things had gone well for him in Mindanao. The job was to hold and pacify the territory where a largely Muslim population resided and reduce their ability to provide clandestine support to the insurgency. He actually enjoyed fighting, and for a while kept a list of his kills. But before long, the Moro patrols knew enough not to venture into the Rangers' sector, and things got quiet.

Bongo had recognised another opportunity, one that would earn him more money than the government was paying. All it took was a little leaning on the locals, and they were more than happy to fill his pockets if it meant they wouldn't be harassed by him and his men. It worked out well for all involved. At least it did until three years earlier, with the fall of the Marcos government and the arrival of that bitch Corazon Aquino.

Up to that point, he'd operated almost with impunity. On a couple of occasions, he'd been put up on charges, once for beating an elderly shop owner half to death, and another time for raping a young village girl. The old man had failed to come up with his protection money on time. His fault. When charged, Bongo claimed he found him trying to hide ammunition destined for the insurgents. Easy.

The girl was a different story. Things got sticky over her. Bongo claimed she was a prostitute, and the encounter was consensual. The girl's father turned out to be one of the village elders and the family was well respected, so his allegations about her character were not believed. He was looking at a court-martial and felt certain he would get it. His salvation was that the Cruz family were loyal supporters of the Marcos regime, and a timely call to his father in Manila had resulted in a communication from the President's palace to his commanding officer. Magically, the whole unpleasantness went away.

The winds changed with the new administration. First, when Aquino negotiated a peace agreement with the Islamists, thus putting an end to his extortion racket; then when her administration made sure that military commanders were aligned with her policies.

Bongo began to feel personally threatened. If an accident were to befall him at the hands of his erstwhile victims, he got the distinct feeling that his new superiors would not be put out. Fortunately, the officers of the Scout Rangers were still Marcos loyalists, so he'd been able to wrangle a secondment to his current job at Fort Bonifacio. He had initially hoped there would be some opportunity for graft, but to his chagrin, he found there were too many controls in place over procurement. Before the regime change, there had been talk of his maybe getting a commission, despite having blotted his copybook, but that was never going to happen now. So here he was, stuck behind a desk, with no prospect for advancement. Bored and idle, his potential wasted.

After his shift, Bongo headed north to Quezon City to meet up with some buddies for beers and pool. Booze and girls were cheaper there than in the capital, not that he was looking for a girl right now. One of them had given him a dose of the clap a couple of weeks back and he'd been pissing razor blades while he waited for the antibiotics to kick in.

On top of that, he was under increasing pressure from his family to marry. While deployed, he could evade their nagging to settle down, but now that he was posted close to home, there was a seemingly endless stream of introductions being made to him of "nice girls" from "good families." Initially, it was only his mother piling on the pressure, but more recently, his father had got in on the act, looking to cement his business connections. When the Marcos administration fell, the political patronage for his father's small construction company had dried up as well, and the business had to fend for itself.

Bongo had no patience with the coy courtship rituals local custom demanded. For starters, he didn't only have to show interest in a girl, but in her entire family. And some of the families were immense. A couple of the girls were decent looking, and he would have been happy to bed them, but there would be no chance of that unless he walked them up the aisle. Fatherhood and domesticity might be what everyone else was looking for, but the thought of it left him cold.

The bar was little more than a glorified tin shed with a booming jukebox wedged between the doors leading to the toilets. The music was barely audible above the noise of the electrical generator supplying power to the place.

Metro Manila was plagued with continuous rolling power outages. Anyone who could afford it had a backup generator, and there was a thriving black market for the things. Bars and restaurants simply could not operate without one in the stiflingly hot and humid Philippine climate. One of Corazon Aquino's first acts upon taking office in 1986 had been to cancel the commissioning of the country's first nuclear plant. Now her government was locked in expensive litigation with the American company Westinghouse, claiming the corporation had engaged in corruption and graft on a massive scale, facilitated by the Marcos regime. The government, however, failed to secure replacement energy sources to compensate for the failure of the Bataan plant to go online, leaving the national grid unable to support the burgeoning demands of Luzon, the largest island of the archipelago.

This was just one of the reasons the Aquino government was deeply unpopular with small business owners like Juan Santos, owner of the bar that Bongo and his buddies liked to frequent.

Bongo scowled at the pool table, staring at the last solid he failed to sink. This gave his opponent, Danny Rodriquez, an opening.

"I need another beer," Bongo growled. He looked at the young Filipina seated nearby. "Jasmine, grab me a San Miguel. You can put it on Danny's tab." Bongo looked at Danny as he added the last, hoping to distract him enough to put him off his stroke.

"Fuck you, Bongo." Danny's eyes remained fixed on the pool table as he lined up his shot.

"I barely covered the cost of gas with my jeepney today. I can just about pay for my own beer, let alone fork out for a round for you. The peso is worthless since Aquino and her crowd got in. Soon all it will be good for is wiping my ass."

Jeepneys were the ubiquitous, cheap mode of transport in the Philippines. They were small hop-on, hop-off buses, owner-operated.

Jasmine slid off her chair and went over to the bar where Eddie was already taking the caps off the beers. Danny sank a couple of stripes before missing, which gave Bongo his opportunity to close out the game.

"Aquino has been a disaster," he said, lining up his shot.

"You got that right, Bongo," Eddie chimed in from behind the bar. "Power supply has gone to shit since she came in. It cost me six months of my profits to buy a fucking generator."

Bongo vented his own grievances. "First thing Aquino did was cave to the Muslim fuckers in the south. Of course, she's been in bed with the communists from the get-go. I mean she let that commie Antichrist Sison out, him and three of his henchmen, as soon as she came to power. She's using the communists as a way to rein in the military, or so she thinks. She forgets it's the military that handed her the presidency."

"What do you have to say about it all, Jasmine?" Eddie pulled the girl towards him and gave her a rough kiss as she tried to pass him his beer. Jasmine wriggled out of his grasp with practised ease.

"Cardinal Sin told us to vote for Corazon, so I did." She returned to her perch on the barstool, placing the requested beers on the table before her. "But she has betrayed Our Blessed Mother by allying herself with communists. The president has lost her way. I pray for her daily." She crossed herself piously.

Bongo smiled as three former comrades entered the building with gusto, their voices raised above the din from the jukebox. They were quickly joined by a couple of young girls who appeared as if on cue from a backroom. There was a lot of backslapping and good-natured ribbing among the Ranger veterans. The pool table was in high demand. Those waiting their turn passed the time playing darts.

Bongo sorely missed the camaraderie of his old platoon. Sitting behind a desk in Fort Bonifacio was safer, but it was boring as all hell. His mates were still deployed, but as he soon found out, were on a three-day pass from the front. This was their second day, and from the look of them, they hadn't slept the night before. After the initial euphoria of the reunion, conversation inevitably turned to pay and conditions.

"It's all very well for you guys," Bongo said as he sat with his fellow Rangers. They were sharing pulutan, an array of bar food, which had been prepared in the tiny kitchen in the rear. The plates were being constantly replenished by the ever-attentive bar girls as the young men ate. "You at least get the combat pay allowance. I get fuck-all sitting behind a desk."

Joshua Batista, the youngest of them at nineteen, snorted. "Even with the allowance, as a private I'm getting the equivalent of less than thirty dollars U.S. a month. The peso is worth shit against the greenback, and inflation is through the roof."

"Before her husband got himself shot in the head, Cory Aquino was just a housewife, and that's all she's fit for," Bongo said as he helped himself to a handful of prawn crackers. "She played the part of grieving widow to perfection. She milked Benigno's assassination for all it was worth. The whole country fell for it, and now her plump ass is sitting in the President's palace. The dumb bitch has no idea how to run the country."

"Pool table's all yours, guys," Danny called out. "I have to get back on the streets to earn a few pesos."

Joshua and Ernesto, the other private, stood up and headed for the table. This left Bongo and Andres Soledad, the lieutenant who had been in charge of Bongo's platoon, alone. Soledad was an observer, and tonight was no different. It hadn't escaped Bongo's notice that while the rest of them went on about Aquino and her socialist government, Soledad remained quiet, not once betraying his feelings on the matter.

He was always a tight-lipped motherfucker, Bongo thought, as he met Soledad's appraising stare.

"Interesting posting, Fort Bonifacio," Soledad said, spearing a couple of pork rinds with his fork. "Sort of a military nerve centre."

"It's just a lot of paper-pushing if you ask me." Bongo shrugged.

"Still, they must maintain high security around it," Soledad replied. "Around the clock, I imagine."

"Not as much as you might think," Bongo said, wondering why he cared. "A lot of security during the day to check on traffic in and out, but after office hours there's just a couple of sentries posted at the fort entrances."

"Well, I'm sure you're pretty familiar with the routine of the place, now you've been posted there for over a year." Soledad stroked his chin as he spoke before standing. "I'm in the mood for a round of darts. You in, Bongo?" It was more of an order than a query.

Bongo ran his fingers through his hair. He felt a touch of irrational anxiety. *Why am I suddenly flavour of the month for this asswipe?*

Slowly, he hauled himself to his feet and followed Andres Soledad in the direction of the dartboard.

Chapter Four

Josh Steinberg woke up at 4:00 a.m. feeling ravenous. In short order, he devoured all the chocolate and nuts he could find in the minibar, and the two bananas that were part of the fruit basket in his suite. He then took a shower. Thirty minutes later he was wide awake, jet-lagged, and wondering what he was going to do with himself for the two and a half hours before he met Lou Holt for breakfast.

He tuned in to CNN and was quickly bored. He phoned down to the desk and confirmed that the gym was open twenty-four hours. *Might as well do something productive. The shower was a fucking waste of time.*

Quarter past six found him in the restaurant, sipping coffee and perusing the International Herald Tribune. At 7:00 precisely, a short, squat young man with a crew cut came striding into the restaurant and looked around inquiringly.

Josh briefly rose to his feet. Lou Holt zeroed in and weaved his way with surprising agility through the tables until he reached where Josh was seated. The man appeared to have no neck. His head sat perched on massive shoulders. He looked for all the world like a humanised version of the Transformer action figure that Josh had bought for his nephew's last birthday.

"How ya doing? I'm Lou Holt. Assume you're Steinberg, or if you're not I'm going to look like a right dumbass." The query was rhetorical. Holt deposited his briefcase on a chair and swivelled to look appreciatively in the direction of the buffet table.

"Ah, breakfast. This place does a fantastic spread. All styles of cuisine. It caters to the Westerners, the Japanese, and the locals. For the Filipinos it's rice with everything, chicken, pork, eggs, you name it. Try some of the rice porridge, Arroz Caldo they call it. Tastes a lot better than it looks. Great hangover cure. There's miso soup and all sorts of fish. Pastries are great, and be sure to have some fresh fruit juice. The mango and papaya are all freshly squeezed." Holt was positively salivating. "Let's get loaded up and then I can fill you in on what we have going on here." He barrelled away. Josh had yet to say a word.

The next twenty minutes were devoted to serious eating. Josh had an omelette prepared fresh by a chef at the egg station. He also sampled a small bowl of the rice porridge, just to be polite, and found it surprisingly good. Coffee was continuously replenished by an efficient, older waitress. In the time it took Josh to consume his omelette, his companion had vacuumed his way through three platefuls of food. *He must have some exercise regime to burn off those calories if this is how he eats every day,* Josh thought in amazement.

Finally, Lou Holt's rate of consumption slackened and his running commentary on the varieties of cuisine he was sampling tailed off. If their dietary preferences were in sharp contrast, how the two men were dressed was equally so. Josh wore a suit, tie, and wingtip leather shoes. Lou Holt had on a sort of embroidered shirt, slacks, and slip-on loafers. Once sated, he seemed more inclined to pick up on social cues, and noted Josh's quizzical expression as he fingered his tie.

"I imagine you're wondering what sort of fancy dress this is I'm wearing for a business breakfast? The shirt is a Barong. It's formal Filipino attire. It's an acceptable alternative to a suit, well suited to the climate here. You don't sweat nearly as much. All the local staff wear them. Nearly all the guys that get posted here from Stateside switch to them if they're staying any length of time. I look good in one, don't you think?" Lou patted his stomach contentedly.

"It makes a statement that's for sure. Since I feel I'm slowly melting here even with the air conditioning, I think I'm going to be in the market for a barong myself before long." Josh gave Lou a wry smile.

"OK, hotshot, I'm not sure what line of bullshit the guys back in Boston fed you, but let me fill you in on what the real state of play is in this little neck of the woods." Lou rubbed his forehead and leaned forward, arms on the table.

"Our company, Emerald Systems, bought themselves a midsize Australian IT software services company, Bondi Ltd., a couple of years back. Bondi had themselves a data centre here in Manila which handled their back-office systems, payroll, human resources, accounting, and the like. Nice peaceful operation, two IBM system 38 minicomputers and thirty staff all told. Emerald decides it's more economical to outsource all that shit going forward. The original plan was to shut the Manila data centre down. Then some genius back at Corporate decides Emerald needs to get on the offshore processing bandwagon. You know the idea, we can write computer programs for you, Mr Customer, for half the price you're paying in the U.S. by shipping the specs overseas to cheap Asian locations. The Board buys in and then there's even better news. Emerald doesn't have to go set up a centre cold turkey. We already have one. Picked it up as part of the Bondi acquisition. We leverage that and we're off to the races. There's a slight fly in the ointment though. Emerald customers are big IBM mainframe types. There's not much call for System 38 expertise. Not to worry. Emerald will upgrade the Manila operation, lease itself an IBM 370—oh, and by the way build out the air-conditioned clean room one of these suckers requires. The Emerald sales reps go gangbusters, the contracts come rolling in. It's all just ducky. There's just the small matter of delivering the code over here in Manila."

Holt paused and grinned evilly. "It's been a shit show from the get-go. First of all, there's a reason the place relied on the System 38s. They take no care and feeding. You switch them on in the morning and away you go. An IBM mainframe is a totally different animal. You need systems programmers, operations staff, a pristine environment. Otherwise, it throws up all over itself. I was parachuted in here six months ago to sort out the availability problem. When I arrived, the fucking mainframe was down half the time. Now we have eighty-five per cent availability, which is still piss poor by normal standards but light years better than what they were dealing with. The other problem is programmer productivity. It's like thirty per cent of what we would expect back home. We had planned on a headcount of fifty for the offshore operation here. Now we're at a hundred and counting. We're running two shifts a day seven days a week to maximise utilisation of the mainframe. This is where you come in, sunshine. Management is looking to you to get productivity up. You'll meet Mark Webster, he's in charge of this whole operation when you get in. He'll give you a sugar-coated version of what I just said, but I figured I could level with you once I saw you chowing down on the Arroz Caldo just now like I told you to."

Josh had been hanging on Lou Holt's every word. "I really appreciate the candour, Lou. I could spend days, if not weeks spinning my wheels trying to figure all this out for myself."

"Don't get too carried away, pal," was Lou's cynical rejoinder. "I've told you what the problem is, but fixing it means figuring out how to light a fire under the local workforce. Good luck with that."

"I'm not sure I follow," Josh said, feeling anxious.

"We need to get over to the office," Lou replied, looking at his watch. "Webster will be wondering where you are. I'll take you out on the town tonight and show you the nightlife. I can give you more of the lowdown then."

When Josh and Lou exited the hotel, Lou slipped twenty pesos to one of the bellboys who sprinted off down the street. "I sent him to fetch my driver," he explained. "Things are dirt cheap here if you're on a U.S. salary, not to mention the out-of-town living allowance. It means I can pay for my own chauffer. Great perk after you've gone and got yourself shitfaced of an evening. The budget runs to lots of other services too," he added cryptically with a slight smile.

It was a twenty-minute drive through a maze of backstreets to the data centre. Lou Holt's driver was taciturn, but obviously knew his way around the city. Josh was a little startled to find the reception manned by two armed security guards.

"More for show than anything else," Lou told him dismissively. "I'm not sure how much use they'd be in a real scrap. They didn't bother with any of this before the takeover. Our bossman Webster is a bit of a pussy, if you ask me. He's forever having staff meetings about preserving employee safety. He and his wife live in a heavily guarded, gated community down near the bay."

Mark Webster turned out to be a heavyset man in his mid-forties with a corner office replete with Red Sox memorabilia. He seemed homesick to Josh, asking eagerly for all the local news about Boston and being particularly anxious to have a postmortem on the rather undistinguished season of the city's baseball team. Josh took no interest in baseball, preferring football and basketball, and struggled to engage with Webster on what was one of his favourite topics.

I'm going to need to bone up on off-season Red Sox news, he thought ruefully.

The morning was taken up with a tour of the facility and a mind-numbing round of introductions. By lunchtime, Josh could scarcely keep his eyes open. The coup de grâce was delivered at the shift handover status meeting, which took place mid-afternoon. As Lou Holt had said, there were two ten-hour programming shifts a day to maximise use of the mainframe. The hours between midnight and four were reserved for the systems programmers to do backups and software updates.

What seemed a small army of people crammed into a conference room to do the handover. Josh was confronted with a myriad of spreadsheets which detailed various metrics of progress or lack thereof in programming and testing the various software application contracts. He found himself drifting in and out of consciousness as Holt kicked him surreptitiously under the table from time to time to keep him awake. The meeting dragged on interminably. His overall impression was that an inordinate amount of time was devoted to personnel issues. So and so was out sick or had a family funeral, which meant they were unable to complete their assignment. Of the twenty people in the room only about half said anything, which got

Josh to wondering why the other half were there in the first place. Finally, it was over.

"So, what did you think of the daily status clusterfuck?" Lou Holt asked Josh as they left the conference room.

"I couldn't take much in, to be honest, Lou. The jet lag is really doing a number on me. I'm going to have to go back to the hotel and get some sleep. I'm about to pass out," Josh confessed. "As a status meeting, it didn't manage to give me much sense of exactly where we are against schedule. But that may be because I'm out to lunch right now."

"No pal, you got it sussed OK," Holt told him. "We're about two months behind schedule, give or take, and 50 per cent over budget. Me, I keep score on the back of an envelope."

"Holy shit," Josh said. "What does Mark Webster do all day long if that's the case?"

"When he's not worried about being kidnapped and held for ransom or sold for spare parts?" Lou Holt sneered, but then got sincere again. "Webster runs a lot of interference to keep the local bureaucrats off our back. There's a lot of permitting and local labour law stuff to keep straight. Also he spends a shitload of time managing the expectations of our not very happy customers. He's not hard-nosed enough for this gig. That's just the long and short of it. I'll have my driver drop you back at the Peninsula so you can get some sleep. I'll swing by around eight this evening. We can have dinner and then head out to see the nightlife."

Josh did not feel remotely interested in a night out on the town, but Lou Holt had befriended him, and he did not want to risk pissing him off by coming across as antisocial.

"That would be great, Lou. I appreciate the ride. I'm sure I'll be fine with a couple of hours' shuteye."

After several hours of a deep dreamless sleep, Josh, refreshed, joined Lou Holt for dinner in the Peninsula Hotel restaurant. Both men opted for steak washed down with an expensive Australian cabernet. Josh rarely drank wine, but Holt revelled in discussing the selection with the sommelier and was aghast when Josh initially suggested he might prefer a beer.

"You can't have beer with a prime cut of fillet mignon. I'm clearly going to have to take your education in hand, young Steinberg."

There was in fact only two years in age difference between the two, Josh learned. Lou was from Nebraska and had enlisted in the Army at age eighteen. He'd had postings in Seoul and Okinawa, which had given him a taste for life in Asia. Taking full advantage of the GI Bill, he got a degree in IT after his discharge, and when the opportunity in Manila presented itself, he had grabbed it with both hands. The conversation over dinner allowed the two Americans to get to know each other and swap stories about their high school and college days. Josh was keen to get some more background about his new working environment, but Lou soon expressed irritation over continuing to talk shop.

"You'll get the hang of the place soon enough, Josh. It'll happen by osmosis. Don't be such a Dudley Do-Right, for Chrissake. We're out on the town. Let's have some fun. First though, we have to finish dinner with a cigar."

Josh was dubious. "I'm not a cigar smoker, Lou."

Lou grinned knowingly. "Believe me, buddy, you want a cigar."

He beckoned to a stunningly beautiful Filipina who hovered in the background with a trolley containing liqueurs and a very large humidor. She approached their table with graceful ease and positioned herself and the trolley strategically between them.

"Two of your best for me and my friend here. We'll leave you to choose." Holt looked her squarely in the eye.

She returned his gaze steadily. "Of course, sir."

Languorously, she opened the humidor and began the selection of a cigar. She ran the back of a fingernail along the length of a couple of them and then, selecting one, she began to roll it gently between her fingers, maintaining eye contact with Holt all the while. She held it to her ear and listened for the crackle of the wrapping. Satisfied with the sound it made, she deftly cut the top off and proffered it to him. Lou Holt clenched it firmly between his teeth, grinning broadly. Using an ornate lighter, she then allowed him to inhale until the end of his cigar glowed red. It was an erotic ritual, so much so that when she turned her attention to Josh, he found himself getting an involuntary hard-on, and blushed red in embarrassment.

He was grateful for the overhang of the linen tablecloth and the dim lighting.

Holt tipped the girl extravagantly after she had topped off her performance by supplying each of them with an expensive cognac in Waterford cut-glass tumblers. Josh took a few puffs of the cigar for form's sake, but in truth, it was making him feel nauseous. He was relieved when Lou stubbed his out half-smoked and put the rest of it in his pocket.

"Finish it later," he said. "Now to sample a few of the clubs on Burgos Street. We stay at each one until the first 'I love you.'"

"Say what?" Josh exclaimed. "I don't understand."

"You will," Lou said, and bounded to his feet.

Their first port of call on Burgos Street was Bojangles. The doormen clearly knew Lou Holt and waved him and Josh through without incident. It took Josh's eyes a couple of minutes to adjust to the dimly lit interior, which was crescent-shaped with rings of concentric small tables cascading down to a central dance floor. Four stools surrounded each table. The decor was red brocade wall hangings and curtains. The brightly illuminated dance floor was in sharp contrast to the seating area, which was lit with a single small lamp placed on each table. Lou had a short negotiation with the Jamaican, and they were shown to their place halfway back, from where several patrons were gyrating to disco tunes being played by a disc jockey.

"You're going to need to choose a girl for the evening as your companion," Lou explained to Josh. "That's the drill here. She'll try to get you to buy her Champagne. Ignore her. Offer to buy her a glass of the house wine. Otherwise, you'll end up with a bill running into the hundreds of dollars if you're not careful."

A girl came up to them and perched herself on the stool beside Lou. "Hello Louis, I haven't seen you here for a while. I've missed you."

Lou grabbed her firmly by the waist. "Hello, Rosa. Have you been behaving yourself? This is my friend, Josh."

Rosa gave Josh a practised coquettish smile. As if by magic, two San Miguels and a white wine spritzer had appeared on the table.

"You're going to have to choose a girl of your own," Lou said as he surveyed the dance floor. On cue, a stunningly beautiful Filipina glided up and put her hand lightly on Josh's arm.

"Would you like to buy me a drink, sir?" she asked.

Josh was flattered and excited all at once. Back home in the singles bars he used to frequent, a girl as stunning as this would be way out of his league. He was just about to ask her what she fancied when Lou leaned over and whispered in his ear.

"You don't want that one. Or maybe you do." Lou shrugged. "That's a she-boy you're talking to."

Josh looked confused.

"He's a transvestite," Lou explained. "Rule of thumb. If the 'girl' has broader shoulders than you or is the same height as you, it's a guy."

Josh was nonplussed. The idea that he could have been attracted to another man was unsettling. Brusquely, he removed the hand from his arm. "I don't think so," he said firmly.

Lou and Rosa exchanged an amused and knowing look. In the end Josh settled for a big-breasted companion two feet shorter than himself.

The clientele liked to dance and were good at it. At one point, the entire dance floor took to performing the Electric Slide, and could easily have passed for a professional dance troupe.

Squarely in the middle of the dancers were two men dressed in identical white suits. There was an obvious family resemblance, and Josh could only conclude that he was looking at a father and son. The younger man could not have been more than twenty.

What sort of degenerate takes his son dancing in a glorified whorehouse? We sure as hell are not in Kansas anymore.

His companion for the evening was becoming steadily more intimate. They danced together a couple of times. The beers kept coming, and he was getting tipsy. After one particularly hot and heavy dance, she positioned herself between his legs as he sat on his stool, kissed him, and said, "I love you, Josh."

A hand clapped his shoulder.

"And we're out of here," Lou said briskly. "Let's go sample the delights of the Paradise Club."

It all became a blur. Josh could not remember how many bars they visited. It was after one in the morning when Lou and his driver dropped him off at the hotel. Pissed drunk, he managed to find his hotel room and passed out fully clothed on the bed.

Chapter Five

Josh was woken at 7.00 a.m. by the incessant ringing of the phone beside his bed. He came to consciousness through a blinding headache and a mouth that felt as if it was stuffed with cotton wool. Initially he had no idea where he was. The heavy curtains on his windows kept the hotel room in total darkness, even though the sun had already risen. Only the flashing of the red light on the telephone oriented him. With difficulty, he put the receiver to his ear.

"Your wake-up call, Mr Steinberg. It is shortly after 7.00 a.m. I hope you have a nice day, sir."

Josh felt sick to his stomach. He wanted to throw up.

I've destroyed myself, he thought despairingly. *And on a weeknight, too. How am I going to get through the day?*

By the time he arrived at the office, a full half hour late, everyone else was already at their desks. Josh slipped into his chair, in what he hoped was an unobtrusive manner, and made a show of perusing some reports before the status meeting he was supposed to chair in his new role as application programming manager. Waves of nausea swept over him at regular intervals. With difficulty, he jotted down some pointed queries he intended to make at the meeting. *I need to show I know my stuff,* he thought as he drank yet another bottle of water.

The effort to stay hydrated meant several trips to the bathroom. During one, he encountered Lou Holt, who seemed none the worse for his night on the town. Looking around furtively, Josh determined that there was no one else in the washroom.

"I feel like crap," he confessed.

"That's because you drank too much," Lou said as he washed his hands.

"You were downing beers at a clip too, Lou," Josh protested.

"Two things, old buddy." Lou moved to the towel rack. "One, I'm about a hundred pounds heavier than you; and two, you let the bar staff hustle you into buying more than you normally would. I was nursing my drinks and you weren't. You'll get the hang of things, never fear." He smiled and clapped Josh heartily on the back. Josh winced. "Look on the bright side. You didn't get so wasted you ended up in bed with that bar girl. Cheer up, it's Friday. You can practice newfound moderation when we go out tonight."

Josh was aghast. "You're crazy if you think I'm going to have a repeat of last night, Lou. It will be all I can do to get through the day."

Lou was unfazed. "Bullshit. You need to get back on the horse. Anyway, all I'm suggesting is a quiet evening at my favourite bar. The nightclubs are for the tourists and the short-stay guys. If you're going to spend any time here it's a different setup. I just took you out last night to show you some of the local colour. I never go clubbing myself unless I'm showing someone the sights."

"Thanks," Josh mumbled.

"Come on, champ. Don't be a wimp. It'll be a nice relaxing time. I'll introduce you to my live-in girlfriend."

In spite of himself, Josh felt intrigued. "I'll see how I'm feeling later this afternoon."

"That's the spirit. See you at the status meeting."

The meeting got off to a late start. The various team leaders ambled in at five or ten minutes past the hour. They then proceeded to chat about family, upcoming social or sporting events, anything and everything, it seemed, besides work. With difficulty, Josh suppressed his growing irritation. Finally, fifteen minutes late, he convened the meeting.

There were seven applications under development at the centre. Only one of them was on schedule and on budget, and that was only because the timeline had been revised to account for slippages the week before. Josh had decided in advance of the meeting that he would make his presence felt when it came to the report from the project furthest behind.

The project leader, a thin man in his thirties with thick glasses and a receding hairline, gave the by now familiar litany of excuses for poor performance: key personnel were out sick, the program specifications sent from the U.S. had not been clear enough, testing had taken longer than anticipated.

Josh interrupted. "These excuses are all well and good, Jose. It is Jose, isn't it? But the hard facts of the matter are that you and your team have slipped a further two weeks behind schedule, and are an additional two hundred days over budget. All of this in the space of a week. We might have done better if you and your crew hadn't bothered to come to work at all."

There was a stunned silence in the room. The object of Josh's ire hung his head and refused to make eye contact. The other participants, with the exception of Lou Holt, studied the papers in front of them. Josh registered the look of consternation and bemusement Lou threw in his direction. He got the uneasy feeling that he had just made a major faux pas, but pushed on.

"We are going to need much more clarity going forward on why schedules and budgets keep slipping. The current reporting criteria are inadequate. I will be meeting with each team individually first thing next week to explain what data I expect to be provided going forward. I don't think there is much more we can accomplish in this session. One point I want to emphasise, however. I expect meetings to start and finish on time. Please make a point of being punctual in your attendance going forward. We're finished here."

They couldn't get out of the room fast enough. A couple of minutes later, only Lou and Josh were left.

"So what is it, Lou?" Josh felt irritated. "You clearly have a beef with how I handled that. I needed them to understand there's a new sheriff in town. Right now the whole thing is a shit show."

Lou remained seated, cracking his knuckles, as he calmly regarded Josh pacing the length of the room back and forth in agitation. "I'm not disputing your assessment, buddy. However, channelling your inner Rambo is not going to improve matters in this environment. You choosing to call poor ol' Jose out in front of his peers like that was a huge loss of face for him. He's not going to show for work Monday, I can tell you that for nothing. If you're lucky, he'll call in sick for a week. If you're not, he'll quit."

Josh stopped pacing. "You can't be serious?"

"I certainly am, you human wrecking ball. The worst of it is, Jose is one of your better supervisors. He was telling the truth when he said the specs coming over from the States were no good. He's the one that figured out the specs didn't do nearly a good enough job of handling exception processing. Easy enough to program the system for when transactions are valid, but you need to be able to detect and properly handle transactions that are not, particularly, as is the case here, when it comes to the credit card business."

"How am I supposed to give negative feedback then?" Josh asked in bewilderment.

"Do it one-on-one, for starters. Also, you need to lose the East Coast edge. These folk have high affiliative needs. You need to put in some time getting to know them. And they you. You can help yourself by losing the suit and tie."

Josh agreed with the last suggestion, if nothing else. He was sweating profusely, and the shirt clung to his back. Suddenly he felt very weary. "I've fucked up, haven't I?" Lou nodded. "What should I do?"

Lou stopped cracking his knuckles. "Some damage control. Invite Jose to lunch. Ask him about his family. His wife just had a baby girl. He's over the moon about it. He has two sons already but he's always wanted a daughter. See where it goes from there. Tomorrow go shopping for some local business attire. Oh, and try smiling a bit more." He shifted gears. "You coming out tonight?"

Josh regarded his colleague with newfound respect and gratitude. "Sure, Lou. I'm game."

"This is my address. Swing by around seven." Lou scribbled the information on a sheet of paper in front of him and passed it to Josh.

Lou Holt lived on a tree-lined street in Legaspi village, one of the more desirable neighbourhoods in Makati. *He does alright for himself,* Josh thought as he knocked on the door.

Lou met him with a beer in hand, which he passed to his guest. "Come right in. We're out back on the porch." As they passed through an airy, tastefully furnished living room, he gestured around the house. "Two bed, two bath bungalow, open plan, bit of a garden, close to the office. Not too shabby, huh?"

"It's a very nice setup alright," Josh agreed with a touch of envy.

"With your salary and out-of-town allowance you should have no problem finding something that suits you. A lot of the expats prefer apartment living, but I find this gives me a bit more privacy."

As they passed through sliding doors he said, "This is Marta. Say hello, Marta."

A young Filipina was curled up in a hammock strung in a corner of the bungalow's back porch. She was reading. Marta had a great figure, but a very sour expression spoiled her otherwise fine features. She looked up at Josh and gave a perfunctory smile before returning to her magazine.

Lou seemed not to notice her ungracious behaviour. "I had Teresa, my daily, prepare us some pulatan. Local heavy hors d'oeuvres, Teresa!" he called out. "Our guest has arrived!"

A squat, middle-aged woman waddled out a couple of minutes later with a tray of appetisers which she spread out on the patio table in front of them. It took her three trips before the complete array of dishes was presented. If Marta was taciturn, Teresa was the opposite. She was cheerful and talkative, engaging Lou in banter as if he were a naughty schoolboy. The arrival of food also brought the girlfriend to life. *She won't keep her figure long if she keeps chowing down like that,* Josh thought. The two men spoke as they ate and Marta made no effort to join in.

"Marta is not a great conversationalist, as you might have noticed," Lou said as he and Josh walked along the street. They were headed to Mogombo, the local bar Lou liked, which turned out to be fifteen minutes away. "But that's not what I keep her for. She's great in the sack and satisfies all my baser needs."

Lou was matter-of-fact. "From a health point of view it's better to make some sort of arrangement with a girl if you're going to be here for a long time. Marta has been live in with me for the past six months. Made her take the HAGS test before I took her on. Had myself checked out while I was at it."

"HAGS test?" Josh was nonplussed.

"Herpes, AIDS, Gonorrhoea, Syphilis," Lou said. "A fair number of STDs knocking about. Just as well you didn't hook up with anyone last night. We would have had to swing by the Australian Embassy to get you a supply of prophylactic penicillin."

"That's very civic-minded of the Australians," Josh said, impressed.

Lou elbowed him in the ribs good-naturedly. "The Embassy's a bar, numb-nuts. You really are wet behind the ears."

Mogombo was cheerful and bright with a Caribbean theme. The bar girls wore tight-fitting, colourful sarongs. There was a constant buzz of conversation. Josh instantly felt more relaxed than he had the night before. For one thing, he wasn't being constantly hustled by the bar staff. Lou was clearly a regular, engaging in easy banter with the other expats hanging out there.

Josh found he was actually enjoying himself for the first time since leaving Boston. He whiled away the time chatting, playing Jenga or liar's dice. He mused about work and resolved that the following week, he would start afresh and make amends for his ham-fisted initial foray into the local environment.

Then he saw her. She must have just come on shift. There was something about her eyes and the way she tilted her head. He felt his chest tighten. Lou was flirting with one of the bar girls. Josh reached over and grabbed his arm tightly to get his attention.

"Who is that girl behind the bar to your left, Lou, do you know?"

Lou swivelled his head around to get a better look. "That's Rita. Nice girl. Bit too thin for my taste. You want to meet her?"

Josh couldn't take his eyes off her. "If I could."

Lou caught the mama-san's attention, and with a couple of practised indications with his head, communicated Josh's interest in Rita. On cue, she drifted toward them and stood beside Josh.

"Hello, I'm Rita. Would you like to buy me a drink?"

"Sure, I'd love to, Rita." Instantly the bartender poured her a glass of wine. "My name is Josh, by the way. I'm new in town and don't know very many people."

She smiled sympathetically. "You sound American. What is Josh short for?"

"Joshua, like the guy from the Bible."

"It's a nice name. Do you mind if I call you Joshua?"

"The way you say it, not at all."

She smiled. For the next hour, he hardly came up for air. She listened to him with rapt attention, and wanted to know all about Boston, what he did for a living, and his impressions of the Philippines. Maybe it was homesickness, maybe the strength of the physical attraction he felt for her, but he couldn't stop talking.

Eventually Lou interrupted their conversation. "I'm going to head back home to Marta, Josh. You're welcome to hang out some more with Rita here if you like." He gave Josh a meaningful look which he did not understand.

Josh suddenly felt anxious about being left alone to fend for himself. "No, Lou. I think I'll leave with you."

"Fair enough. I'll have my driver drop me off and then he can take you back to your hotel. The bill is paid. Say goodbye to Rita."

"Goodbye, Rita. I've really enjoyed talking to you. I'll be back soon, I promise." Feeling like an awkward high schooler, he gave her a peck on the cheek.

"Goodbye Joshua, I hope to see you again soon." She smiled at him warmly, but he could see with a pang of jealousy that her eyes were already surveying the bar.

As they sat in the back of the car Josh quizzed Lou about the encounter. "Why were you giving me that funny look just before we were leaving, Lou?"

"I didn't know whether you wanted to bar fine the girl or not, Josh. That's all."

"Bar fine? What are you talking about?"

Lou hit his head with the side of his hand. "Shit, Josh. I clean forgot about you're being new here. I'll explain."

By the time Lou had explained the bar fine system, Josh was exhausted. "I need my bed. There's just been too much for me to take in."

"Don't sweat it, pal. You'll get the hang of it, never fear." Lou patted him on the arm. "This is me. My driver will leave you at the hotel. See you bright and early Monday morning."

Chapter Six

In the ornate restaurant of the Manila Hotel, Bongo Cruz and Andres Soledad were deep in conversation. Soledad had extended an invitation to Bongo after their dart game the previous week.

This was a rare treat for Bongo. The hotel was the oldest and most prestigious in the Philippines, and the residence of Douglas MacArthur for six years prior to the Japanese conquest in 1941. It was also a favourite venue for Ferdinand Marcos and his wife Imelda before their overthrow. Bongo could remember being taken to the hotel as a child several times, but only as far as the lobby. The outings coincided with political meetings that his father, as a supporter of the Marcos regime, would be summoned to attend. Initially, he had found it all rather boring, but as he moved into his teens, Bongo took a much keener interest in the dignitaries his father pointing out to him, claiming with pride to have made their acquaintance.

This, however, was the first time he had ever dined at the hotel. Indeed, up to this point he had never even had a drink in the place. Bongo was flattered but wary to have received the invitation from Soledad. At one point he even wondered if the man was homosexual and if he was going to be propositioned, but he quickly dismissed that idea when he saw how keenly Soledad appraised the elegant Western women scattered around the dining room. The dinner conversation increasingly focused on politics, and Soledad's interest in finding out where Bongo stood on the Aquino government.

Bongo was initially cautious, and apart from disclosing his family's historic allegiance to Marcos—which he figured was common knowledge anyway—he was careful to provide only guarded criticism of Corazon Aquino. It was an excellent dinner, and Soledad seemed not to mind its expense, ordering a second bottle of vintage Burgundy to go with the Chateaubriand they had agreed to split. As the evening went on, Soledad's own criticisms of the government became increasingly more strident.

"What really pisses me off about this crowd is their policy of appeasement toward the communists. We lost good men fighting those bastards, and now it's all supposed to be forgive and forget."

The outburst came as the men were sipping brandy. Soledad was whispering sotto voce and glancing around him in case they were being overheard. Bongo considered his response. Either Soledad was trying to entrap him, or he meant what he said.

I'm just not that important to be made the target of a sting operation, he thought with a touch of regret.

"I feel just the same as you, Andres, and I think she's wrecking the economy in the bargain. We need to see the back of her."

Soledad eyed him closely. "Would you be willing to do something about that, Bongo?"

Bongo was startled. "How do you mean?"

Soledad placed a hand on Bongo's arm. "Let's go somewhere we can't be overheard. How do you fancy a walk along the bay?"

Bongo considered for a moment, returning Soledad's gaze steadily. "Sure, I'm game."

A cool breeze rolled off the water as they joined locals and tourists strolling along Roxas Boulevard. As he listened to Soledad denouncing the Aquino administration as socialist and degenerate, Bongo revised his opinion of the man. His earlier assessment of him as being reserved and circumspect gave way to the conclusion that he was listening to a nationalist fanatic. After half an hour, Bongo decided he'd had enough.

"I agree with most of what you're saying, Andres, but what exactly do you think I, or you for that matter, can do about it?"

Soledad collected himself and picked up the pace. After a couple of minutes, he said without breaking stride, "A military coup. That's what I'm talking about, Bongo. Led by the Scout Rangers, our regiment."

This guy's a zealot. Following zealots can get you killed.

"Two questions, Andres. What makes you think you can succeed, and where do I fit into this?"

"The military propped up Ferdinand Marcos for over twenty years. It was we who decided he had to go in the end and gave him the shove. The military allowed Corazon Aquino to come to power. We can just as easily take her down."

Soledad stopped under a Balete tree growing on the side of the promenade and turned to face Bongo. To buy himself some time, Bongo lit a cigarette, offering one to his companion, who declined.

"Okay. Let's say I give you that if it's planned right, the military can pull this off. You still haven't told me where I fit in."

Soledad examined a beetle on the trunk of the tree. "I don't know all the details of the operation yet, but I do know we mean to seize control of Fort Bonifacio. It's a stroke of luck you've been posted there."

"If you think I'm going to start blowing things up in the fort you can count me out," Bongo said, agitated at the thought.

"Nothing as dramatic as that," Soledad reassured him. "We just want to know about security. How is it guarded? When do the shifts change? Numbers of men posted at each access point. That sort of thing."

Bongo felt relieved. "That's not so dramatic," he admitted. "I'd still be taking a risk, though, if the coup fails."

"We understand that." Soledad finished his inspection of the beetle. "We would pay you a daily stipend for your effort. Everyone who signs up gets it. Senior commanders merit more, obviously. Call it hazard pay if you will."

"How much?" Bongo asked quickly.

"Fifteen dollars U.S. a day."

"Not a huge amount but better than nothing," Bongo said thoughtfully. "This is a lot to take in, Andres. I'm going to need to think about it."

Andres frowned. "There's not a lot of time, Bongo. If these things are to be done, they need to happen quickly. There's too much risk of discovery the more we delay."

"Give me a day. You'll have your answer tomorrow. We can meet right here."

"I suppose we can manage a day. You know we researched your background pretty thoroughly before we approached you. There's not too much we don't know about you." There was just the slightest hint of menace in Soledad's voice.

Bongo shrugged. "I figured as much. One last question, Andres. Who's leading this coup? Does the guy have what it takes to pull it off?"

"You'll find that out once we know you're with us, Bongo."

"Don't get me wrong here, Andres. I'm loyal to our regiment. I'll follow orders, whatever they turn out to be. I just need to get my head around what you're asking me to do. It's above and beyond, if you know what I mean."

"Tomorrow, same place," Soledad said, clearly unimpressed. He walked over to the curb. The encounter was over. "I'm going to hail a cab."

Bongo lay on his bed, still dressed, in a small, cluttered bedroom of his parents' house, and stared at the ceiling. He went over the events of the evening in his head, trying to replay Andres Soledad's exact words as he debated what to do. There was risk in whichever path he took.

The biggest unknown was how far up the chain of command this plot went. If senior members of the military were involved and he did not cooperate, he was a marked man. It was quite possible he would become a victim of a "training accident." If it was just some disaffected mid-ranking officers, the probability of success was low and his participation in the coup would most certainly be discovered. He immediately discounted the idea of alerting the administration to the plot. He would get no thanks, and he would be a social outcast from his family and friends forever. The money caused him to settle on his course of action. It wasn't that the sum was so large, it was that the conspiracy was well-financed, which suggested that senior figures were involved.

Right now, they just want intelligence. I need to make it as comprehensive as possible. If I tell them about when sanitation trucks make their rounds, when supply deliveries happen, pretty much everything about how the place operates, they'll be content having me do just that and not get any ideas about embroiling me deeper. I need to make myself invaluable to them as a spy. If I'm careful and leave no tracks, I can always deny involvement if this effort fails. If it succeeds, I'm a hero of the revolution. Fuck it, I'm in!

His decision made, Bongo gave himself over to imagining how he could enrich himself under a new regime, which would doubtless be suitably grateful for his efforts.

Chapter Seven

After a week on the job, Josh Steinberg was feeling a lot less like a deer in the headlights. In addition, he was building some rapport with his team managers. As Lou Holt predicted, Jose Ramirez was not at work on Monday, but to Josh's relief, he was at his desk early on Tuesday morning.

Josh went out of his way to be welcoming and cordial, accepting without question the excuse of a family funeral Jose used to justify his absence. He put in place new review checkpoints at key stages of the software building process. Errors were being detected earlier, meaning a cleaner product down the line with less need for costly rework.

Not everything was going well—he discovered that the project completion schedules being communicated to his boss, Mark Webster, were completely unrealistic. It had been left to him to explain that fact, only an hour before, to a stunned and forlorn Webster.

Josh came under pressure from his boss to back off on his assessment, but knowing he would only get one bite at the apple, he dug in his heels and refused to give ground. They agreed that Josh would have freedom to approve overtime, but the revised delivery schedule could not slip further. Webster was left with the thankless task of breaking the bad news to company management, and worse, the customers a few hours later.

Josh was well over his jet lag, installed in a comfortable, one-bedroom apartment in a high-rise half a mile from the office, and he had not touched a drop of alcohol since the fiasco of the previous Friday night. Now he was off to the reflexology centre for a relaxing massage, which would cost him all of ten U.S. dollars.

Once again, he had Lou to thank for introducing him to this incredible amenity. The centre boasted showers, communal hot and cold bathing pools, and a sauna. Patrons hung out on lawn chairs sipping green tea until they were called for their massage, which was performed in a dimly lit room by young Filipinas trained by the centre. The girls' technique was first-rate and uniform. Lou told him that it didn't matter which girl was giving the massage and could attest to that fact personally. This would be his third session of the week.

The place was very popular with Japanese businessmen. You could choose to have either an oil or a pressure massage. Josh opted for the oil-based treatment. Lou warned him that the alternative was excruciatingly painful if you were not used to it. It was also much more physically demanding on the girls. The last part of the session involved the masseuse balancing her client on her hands and feet, using the force of gravity to stretch him. He had seen a 300-pound man contorted in this way by a girl scarcely a hundred pounds herself. On Josh's last visit, he caught a glimpse of the room where the girls rested between customers. Double-decker bunks lined the narrow walls. All were occupied, and everyone looked exhausted. He made sure to tip well.

"They survive on tips," Lou told him. "The centre pays them a pittance. Maybe two bucks a session."

Josh was going to meet up with Lou later at Mogombo. He was hoping to see Rita again. He had been thinking about her all week, unable to get her out of his head. Though it was her trade, the way Rita spoke and how she tilted her head when she listened to him made him feel wanted and special.

Josh made a point of getting to the bar early, hoping Rita would not be monopolised by some other patron by the time he arrived. He was in luck and they settled in at a table in a quiet corner.

"It's nice to see you again, Rita. I really enjoyed our time together last week."

Her face lit up. "I was hoping you would come back, Joshua."

"I did nothing but talk about myself last week. You must think me a real show-off. I know nothing about you, not even your last name or where you're from."

Rita leaned into him and murmured confidentially. "My last name is Cruz. I'm from a small village called Licod on the island of Leyte. It's in the south. I got here a month ago. One of the other bar girls is from my village. She told me about this place. I needed to make some money to help my parents and my younger brother and seven sisters. Eddie, that's my younger brother, is here in Manila. He's staying with our uncle Luis and his wife, Maria. My parents want Eddie to have a good education. It's expensive, though, and they've been worried about not being able to keep up with his fees. I can make good money here and send something back to help them." Rita confessed the last in a rush.

Josh was once again struck by how important family was in this country and how close-knit they were. He thought of his own family. His parents, divorced since he was sixteen, both married again, his mother having recently divorced her third husband, his father working on divorcing his second. A blended family, people called it. A clusterfuck if anyone had asked Josh his opinion. He took every opportunity to avoid family get-togethers.

"Your brother is very lucky to have a sister like you," Josh said, and meant it.

"Eddie will finish high school in two years. Then I can give up this sort of work, Joshua. All the family think I have a job as a live-in maid with a wealthy family here in Manila. Everyone except my cousin Bongo, that is. He's Uncle Luis's son. He dropped by here a couple of weeks ago and recognised me. I begged him not to tell on me and he promised." Anxiety and worry were written all over Rita's face.

Josh frowned. He had asked her a simple question about herself and ended up getting her life story. His thoughts were interrupted by Lou, who clapped him on the shoulder.

"How's it hangin' there, Josh ol' buddy, ol' pal? Let's have a game of darts while I can see straight. You don't mind, do you Rita?"

He's a force of nature, Josh thought ruefully as he excused himself and joined Lou at the dartboard.

The evening passed uneventfully with the usual games of Jenga and liar's dice. There was some comic relief when some newcomers made the mistake of getting into a strip dice contest with a couple of the girls and were soon down to their Y fronts. They were clearly wondering how they were supposed to pay the next forfeit before their companions let them off the hook after a dose of very ribald banter.

After a couple of hours, Josh went to the bathroom. When he came back Lou was on his feet getting ready to leave.

"I'm off for a roll in the hay with my main squeeze, old sport. Enjoy the rest of your evening."

"Where's Rita?" Josh asked, looking around.

"Gone to change. I bar fined her for you. She's yours for the night. If you want to do the nasty with her that's on you, though. I'm not made of money. Enjoy." With that Lou was gone.

Josh stared after him open-mouthed. *What has that lunatic got me into?* The next thing he knew Rita was at his shoulder. Instead of her tight-fitting sarong, she was now dressed in a modest skirt and blouse with a floral scarf around her shoulders, looking for all the world like a pretty young secretary or teacher. She looked up at him expectantly.

"Would you care to go for a walk?" was all he could think of to say.

"That would be lovely." She seemed genuinely pleased with the suggestion.

As they left the bar, she slipped her hand into his. It was a simple gesture of intimacy. Josh squeezed it gently and then put his arm around her waist.

"How would you like a walk around the green belt?" he asked softly.

"That would be very kind of you, Joshua."

It was surprising to her that this young American did not immediately want to take her to his apartment for sex. He claimed he was single, so she could not attribute his hesitancy to guilt. Joshua was considerate of her. Unlike many men at Mogombo, he didn't have his hands all over her. She had yet to figure out if it was because he was new to the scene or if it was innate in him. She hoped for the latter, but for now, she was happy to walk arm in arm with him, just as if they were an ordinary young couple.

As they neared the green belt, they came upon an array of street food vendors. Rita encouraged her companion to sample some of the delicacies. At first Josh was hesitant, but as he saw other Westerners happily eating he became more willing. He sampled cheese sticks and fish balls with her, and seemed to be thoroughly enjoying himself.

A stall to her left caught Rita's eye. She hauled Josh over to it. "Oh Joshua, see, they have Balut, you must try it."

"What is it?" Josh allowed himself to be pulled along by his diminutive companion.

"It's just a cooked egg." He missed the mischievous gleam in her eye.

Josh bought an egg for each of them and bit into his. Something crunched between his teeth. He looked at the half-eaten delicacy and saw the remains of an embryo nestling in the albumen.

"For fuck's sake." He looked around desperately for a serviette so he could spit out what remained in his mouth. "You little vixen!"

She was laughing. "Oh Joshua, don't be such a baby. It's a great delicacy here in the Philippines."

He grimaced. "It's all I can do not to toss my cookies right now, darling. Yech!"

For all his discomfort, Josh took her ribbing in stride. *I'm really happy right now. I think I've fallen in love with the place.*

They strolled along, taking in the sights and sounds of Makati at night and eventually came across a cluster of stalls selling clothing. At Rita's insistence, Josh modelled various Australian bush hats before settling on one that met her approval.

"It will protect you from the sun, Joshua. And it has a string for your chin, so it won't blow off in the wind. That's strong here this time of year, particularly down by the bay. You look very handsome in it."

Josh smiled at the compliment and quite enjoyed the feeling of being minded by her. They stopped to listen to a trio of musicians playing Mozart. Their standard of play was exceptional. Josh casually dropped a five-dollar bill in their basket as he passed on.

Rita marvelled anew at how profligate Americans were with their money. Five dollars was two hundred pesos, a huge tip, when the locals would normally part with maybe ten.

"Oh Joshua, we're just passing the open-air church. Could I just stop a moment and light a candle to the Virgin for my family? I miss them so," Rita pleaded.

"Sure, why not?"

"It will only take me a moment, I promise." She kissed him lightly on the cheek. From a pocket in her dress, she pulled out a black mantilla and scurried off to a statue at the side of the altar.

I get made a present of a call girl for the night and I end up taking her to church. How lame is that?

A few minutes turned out to be ten or more as Rita took time out to chat with some acquaintances. Josh didn't to mind. Time had a different meaning here in the Philippines compared to back in Boston. There everyone seemed to be in a hurry. Here there always seemed to be the opportunity for a chat.

When she returned, they grabbed some ice cream and sat on a park bench. Josh told Rita about his week and the challenges he faced trying to figure out how to connect with her countrymen. She was a good listener. She didn't pretend to understand the details of his job, but she made some very astute observations about the sorts of people he was encountering at work, and what their behaviour signified. They wandered back the way they had come, engrossed in conversation. Almost without realising it, Josh found himself back with her at Mogombo. He fished a fifty-dollar bill out of his wallet and pressed it into her hand.

"I had a great evening, Rita. I really enjoyed myself."

Rita looked in disbelief at the bill he had given her. "But that's an enormous amount, Joshua, and I've done nothing for it."

"You're a working girl, and I'm a satisfied customer. Why don't we leave it at that? Can I see you tomorrow?" He looked at her, his eyes pleading.

"I'd love to, Joshua, but you know I work at the bar."

"If you want to, Rita, I'll square it with the mama-san now. I just wondered if you liked me enough to want to go out with me again?" He stood there awkwardly, waiting for her answer.

"Of course I like you, Joshua. I think you're the kindest, nicest person I've met since I came to Manila."

His face lit up and he kissed her passionately on the lips. She yielded to him. A patron exiting the bar excused himself. They parted, embarrassed. They were in his way.

77

"Okay then, Rita, let me go in here and fix myself up a date." They walked into Mogombo, his arm tightly around her shoulder.

The following evening, Josh examined himself anxiously in the mirror before heading out for his date. Shorts made his legs look too skinny, and anyway, they were still lily white from a New England winter. After a lot of indecision, he finally settled for Chinos, a short-sleeved shirt with an open collar, and a pair of sneakers. No amount of coaxing would get his shock of black, curly hair to stop sticking out all over the place. He wanted Rita to think him handsome. It was ridiculous, of course. He was paying for her company, but he couldn't help himself.

She was waiting for him at the side door of the bar when he got there. She wore a white blouse over a sarong and had a white flower pinned in her dark, silky hair. He was enchanted as he embraced her. The scent of the bloom invaded his senses, redolent with the spirit and character of the exotic land in which he found himself.

"The scent is wonderful," he murmured.

"It's the Rosal. I think you call it Gardenia," Rita said.

He took her to dinner at a buffet-style fish restaurant popular with the locals. It was brightly lit and noisy, with a constant hum of conversation from patrons seated at tables crowded on top of one another in a vast dining space. Rita took delight in explaining the various dishes, what variety of fish was being used, and what sauces accompanied them. A couple of hours passed as they chatted about life in Manila, the busy streets, the noise, the crazy traffic. Josh kept

Rita amused with tales of trying to use the public transportation system and ending up hopelessly lost each time he ventured out.

"I don't suppose you'd like to see where I live, Rita? It's not far from here," he asked. He had chosen the restaurant for precisely this reason, and tried to sound casual in his invitation.

Rita had been waiting for an overture like this. It was inevitable. *I really like him though,* she thought. It would make going to bed with him tolerable.

Josh's apartment had fine views of the city in one direction and overlooked the bay in another. Rita was surprised at how neat he kept it until he explained he had maid service every other day. She marvelled anew at the extravagance of his expat lifestyle. So much living space for just one person. They went out onto his balcony and split a bottle of white wine as they watched the lights of the tankers moored in the huge harbour. As they lingered over the last glass, Josh made his pitch.

"I really enjoyed this evening, Rita. I'd like you to stay over. We don't have to, you know, do anything, unless of course you want to. I'll pay you just the same either way." He looked at his feet as he finished, one hand running nervously through his unruly hair.

He really is a sweet boy. But how long is he going to stay interested in me if I don't have sex with him? Rita thought. *But I want to.*

She walked slowly over to where he was standing and kissed him gently on the lips.

The next morning, Josh awoke to find her showered, dressed, and getting ready to quietly leave. "Where are you going, Rita?" he asked, bewildered.

"I have to get back to the bar, Joshua. I've been out all night. They'll be worried about me."

"But I don't want you to go. Is it a question of money?" He leaned out of the bed and groped for his pants discarded on the floor.

"Joshua, I could only stay with you for the night. That was the arrangement. I have a job I need to keep. At some point you will return to the United States. This is where I live."

He stared at her, open-mouthed. "I thought we had something, Rita." He pulled himself up on the pillows and stared at her for a long moment. Then he said decisively, "Okay, I get it. You don't know me from a hole in the wall. How about this? You keep the job, but I bar fine you every night and you come stay here with me."

She sat down heavily on the bed and looked at him, incredulous. "But that's incredibly expensive, Joshua."

"I don't care. I want to be with you. Of course, I'll pay you for your services as well," he added hastily.

Rita heard the voice of the mama-san in her head. *They'll tell you they're in love with you and forget all about you as soon as they get on the plane home. Don't get emotionally involved with the customers if you want to last in this business.*

She reached over and took his hand. "You wouldn't have to pay me for doing something I want to do, Joshua."

"But you won't go with another guy... I mean *be* with him. I don't think I could stand it." Josh looked at her, feeling anxious.

She touched his cheek and looked him squarely in the eye. "No, Joshua, as long as I'm with you I won't go to bed with any other man."

He pulled her to him and embraced her fiercely. They nestled there for several moments, with the bright morning sun streaming through the window. Reluctantly she made as if to go.

"Give me ten minutes to shower," Josh said, swinging his feet onto the floor. "I'll drop you off on my way to work. What time do you get off tonight?"

"Since you will be taking care of me..." It was a nice euphemism for his paying her bar fine. "I could leave around eleven. I should have made some decent tips by then."

As their taxi weaved its way slowly through the rush hour traffic, Josh looked out the window, watching the young women on the sidewalk, parasols already open against the fierce tropical sun. There was the customary haze of pollution in the air. *I feel so alive today,* he thought. *Coming over here was the best decision I've ever made.*

When they reached the bar, he got out and ran around to open the door for her. Rita was touched by the courtly gesture and gave him a kiss.

"I'll be waiting outside for you at eleven," Josh said.

Rita was surprised. "You don't need to do that, Joshua. I can find my way to your apartment."

"I want to, Rita. I want you to be safe," he said simply.

"Okay then, until tonight, mahal ko." He looked at her quizzically.

"It means my love," Rita said shyly. Josh's face beamed with pleasure as she ran into Mogombo.

Chapter Eight

The alarm went off at 11:30 p.m. Josh opened his eyes reluctantly, roused from a deep slumber. He headed for the bathroom to quickly shower and brush his teeth before heading off to meet Rita outside Mogombo. Her shift never finished earlier than midnight and could go as late as 3 a.m. on weekends. Rita had been living with him less than a week when he realised that if he was going to see anything of her and still manage to hold down his job, he would have to nap in the evenings. There was no way he could function on four hours of sleep a night and she didn't go to bed until 4 a.m. at the earliest. So here he was, getting ready to loiter outside her place of work like some lovesick teenager every night so he could escort her home. He couldn't even ask much about her shift. What was he going to say?

How many guys did you cosy up to tonight honey? How many groped you or tried to get their tongue down your throat?

The thought consumed him with jealousy and self-loathing. He was jealous of the men she pandered to and loathed himself for needing—no, *wanting*—a fucked-up relationship like this.

The conversation on this particular evening followed predictable, mundane lines. He might have been picking up a sales assistant from a department store. Rita had changed into her demure street attire.

"I'm sorry I'm a bit late Joshua, the food order for my last client was late and I had to keep him entertained while we waited for it. Have you been here long?" She looked at him anxiously.

"I just arrived, Rita" Josh lied. He had been waiting forty minutes, occasionally catching a glimpse of her in her skimpy dress, pressed up against a flabby middle-aged man when the door to the bar swung open to allow customers, all male, to enter or leave. He tried to avoid looking at the door, promising himself each night he wouldn't, but he couldn't resist the chance of seeing her. He turned and waved an arm to beckon the taxi he had come in, which was waiting for him. Rita thought it extravagant to be paying someone to hang about when taxis were so plentiful, but Josh felt more secure with a driver he knew.

"Got to keep your wits about you in this town pal," Lou had cautioned him. "Otherwise, you could find yourself waking up on the side of the road minus a kidney. Donor organs are fetching a good price these days." So Josh stuck with the same two or three guys whenever he needed ferrying around town.

The ride home was short, no more than ten minutes. Rita speculated happily about which meat to use in the pancit dish she would prepare for their supper. Pancit was the Filipino word for noodles. Rita liked to use pork, which was cheap, but Josh did not much care for it. It was not a question of religion; he just didn't like the taste. After some discussion, they settled on chicken.

Their life together was a picture of domestic harmony. Since Rita had arrived, there were always fresh flowers in the apartment. She did his laundry and gave it to him when he left his clothes lying around the floor. She listened sympathetically when he bitched about what was going on at work. Rita was smart. He was surprised how quickly she grasped and was able to follow the twists and turns involved in software development. She became truly engaged when he filled her in with the gossip of who was going out with whom, whose wife was going to have a baby, whose birthday it was. He gave her credit for prodding him to take an interest in his fellow workers.

With the benefit of her shrewd insights and observations, he came across as more empathetic at work, and he gave her a lot of credit for softening the take-no-prisoners style of interaction he had adopted at the outset. It was paying off, he had to admit. His team were more open and upfront about problems they were having, which allowed him to get to grips with them before they spiralled out of control. Most of all, he realised he wasn't lonely or homesick since Rita had moved in.

Apart from the fact I'm shacked up with a working hooker, things couldn't be peachier.

"Let's get out of the city this weekend," he said after they finished cleaning up after supper. "We can go to Anilao." Anilao was a popular beach resort about sixty miles from Manila.

"I have to go into work early on Saturday," Rita said.

"Fair enough. Sunday then."

Rita was apologetic. "I need to go to Mass, Joshua, and my uncle and aunt will expect me for dinner."

"For Pete's sake, Rita. I don't see this obsession with Mass given your line of work. If you took your religion seriously you wouldn't be a fucking bar girl."

"If I wasn't a fucking bar girl as you put it, Joshua, we would never have met," Rita said, her good humour vanished.

Josh could see he had touched a nerve and hastened to make amends. "Sorry, I shouldn't have said that. How you practice your religion is between you and your God. I'm the last guy who should be getting up on a soapbox. I'm just disappointed we don't seem to be able to do some fun things together."

Her face softened and she regarded him affectionately. "It's okay. I forgive you." Rita paused and thought for a moment. "I know. I can go to the vigil Mass before I start work and I'll phone my aunt and tell her I have a very bad cold and I'm afraid of giving it to her. A day out at Anilao will be marvellous. Something to look forward to."

"What say we turn in for the night?" Josh said.

Rita looked surprised. "Why are you tired? I thought you napped earlier."

"Not tired exactly." Josh looked at her suggestively. She caught his meaning and smiled.

"You go on ahead. I'll just take a quick shower before I join you."

Josh nodded and gave her a grin, but inwardly he sighed. This was her ritual before and after sex. It was one of the tricks of her trade. She had never once asked him to shower before lying with him. It was not something you asked a *John* to do.

It's no big deal, he thought to himself, but it bothered him all the same. Just another indicator of the ambiguity of their relationship.

They set out early enough on Sunday for their trip to the beach. Josh elected to drive himself and had rented a car for the day. He could not bring himself to follow Lou's example and maintain his own personal chauffeur. It seemed a wanton extravagance. Getting used to the chaotic traffic in Manila was a test of his nerves.

After collecting his rental the night before he had almost chickened out before he even got as far as his apartment and was sorely tempted to turn right around and take the vehicle back to the agency. Only his pride kept him from doing so. He had been foolish enough to tell Lou of his plans to drive himself. His friend had been dubious.

"Driving in this town is not for the nervous, buddy," Lou said.

"If I can handle Boston traffic, I can do this," Josh had responded airily. Now he regretted his bravado.

Rita noticed that Josh was on edge as he wove his way through the melee of cars, bicycles, mopeds, jeepneys, and pedestrians. "Are you sure you want to deal with all this traffic Joshua? It's a long way to Anilao and back and you've had a busy week."

"I'm perfectly fine, Rita," Josh said sharply. "If you want to be useful you could help with directions for getting out of the city."

Even on my day off I end up pandering to some man's endless needs, Rita thought.

She took stock of where they were and managed to give him clear and accurate instructions on how to get out to the highway. Once he was on the straight road Josh visibly relaxed, his grip on the steering wheel easing noticeably.

"Thanks for the help back there. I didn't expect you to know the city streets so well." He took his eyes off the road for a moment to smile at her.

"I have a pretty good sense of direction and I remember my uncle driving us to Anilao last year."

Rita was relieved his good humour had returned. Joshua was a kind man but, like nearly all the Westerners she met, very spoiled. They were easily put out when things didn't go their way. Still, it was very pleasant to be driving in the countryside with no responsibilities or obligations, and she was grateful to him for making it possible.

"So, are you looking forward to your first snorkelling adventure?" Josh asked, breaking her train of thought. "It's what the place is known for, that and the scuba diving."

"I'm a little nervous Joshua. I've never done it before."

"There's not a lot to it, really. You don't even have to be a particularly good swimmer. Just so long as you can float."

"Oh, I can swim well enough but just the thought of having a mask over my face and sticking my head under the water…"

"It'll be great, you'll see."

Josh was not willing to entertain any misgivings. In the end Rita found she really did enjoy the whole experience. It was an expensive pastime and most Filipinos wouldn't dream of paying the inordinate rental fees.

The Sunday evening traffic was heavy, and it took them nearly two hours to get home. Josh was relaxed and the slow going didn't seem to bother him. He passed the time by telling her about Martha's Vineyard, where his parents had brought him and his brother and sister on vacation every summer before their divorce. It was the first time he had spoken of his family with anything like fondness. His previous cryptic references to them had been tinged with bitterness and resentment.

"It's nice to hear about the happy times you had as a boy. You all seemed to get along back then. I understand about the divorce and your parents but why did you fall out with your brother and sister?"

"Kids tend to take sides in a divorce. Ben and Miriam took Dad's side and I felt sorry for Mom. Sure, she had the affair, but he's a cold bastard. I could understand her needing to look elsewhere for companionship. Besides, he was a total shit when it came to the settlement."

He had never been so open with her before. His voice was tinged with sadness as he spoke, eyes fixed on the road, not glancing at her. His lovemaking that night was more affectionate somehow. Afterwards, as she lay in his arms, she heard him murmur softly, "I wonder if you'd like Boston Rita. It's okay in the summer, but it can be a bitch of a winter there."

She felt her heart race. It was the first time he'd ever alluded to the possibility of her going to the States with him. "If I have you with me, I don't think the weather is going to bother me, Joshua."

He chuckled. "You say that now. Anyway, I've been thinking it would be fun to show you the sights."

She pressed herself more closely against him. "I'd really love to do that with you. When could we go?"

"I'm not sure," he answered lazily. "We could go when my stint here is over, or if they extend me, I'll be given a trip back home at some point."

"It sounds very exciting. I'd need a little notice though. I'd have to get a visa."

"Oh that," Josh said. "I'd forgotten you'd need one of those. Sure thing, honey. I'll give you the heads-up in good time. Right now, I need some shuteye though." He gave her a peck on the forehead and rolled over onto his side.

Rita sighed. Joshua lived in his privileged world and still had little comprehension of the challenges and obstacles the locals faced. Still, she obviously meant something to him if he was willing to share part of his life in the United States with her. She closed her eyes and allowed herself to dream.

Chapter Nine

The alarm beside Eddie Cruz's bed went off at 5:30 a.m., and the 16-year-old boy quickly silenced it so as not to disturb his uncle and aunt. He lay in the darkness for a little while, listening to the crickets, interspersed with traffic noise as the city stirred into life. Then, hopping out of bed, he went to a small chest in the corner and pulled out his work clothes: shorts, a T-shirt, and a scarf. There was a sack to hold what he collected, and a thin metal pole to help him sift through the rubbish.

It was Saturday morning, and Eddie was heading out for Smokey Mountain, the vast municipal garbage dump. He worked every weekend as a waste picker. It helped pay for his board while he went to school in Manila. He wrinkled his nose as he got dressed. His clothes stank of garbage even though he washed them every Sunday night. His body also stank after a weekend on the dump, and no amount of washing could entirely remove the putrid smell. He was self-conscious in class every Monday morning, knowing his classmates could detect the lingering odour that seemed to exude from his pores.

At this hour of the morning it was a half-hour jeepney ride to the dump; later in the day that could easily stretch to two. When he arrived it was already crowded with hundreds of people. An endless stream of trucks took turns discharging their load. The pickers rushed and clambered over one another to secure the choicest morsels. Men, women, and children, some as young as six or seven, vied to be first in line, wading knee-deep in the garbage, most of them barefoot. Eddie joined in the melee, nimbly manoeuvring himself to the front.

He was foraging for scrap metal. There was an informal hierarchy among the pickers. He wasn't senior enough to be allowed to hunt for precious metals. Scrap metal paid better than plastic, though, so he considered himself lucky. It was backbreaking work and dangerous as well. Recently a young boy had suffocated when he failed to get out of the way of one of the trucks tipping its garbage onto the vast pile. There was also the risk from medical waste, intermingled with all the other trash. Used syringes and dressings were scattered underfoot.

By nine o'clock, the temperature was in the 80s, and today there was no breeze to dissipate the toxic vapours that rose from the dump, burning his lungs and stinging his eyes despite the scarf covering his nose and mouth. Eddie worked single-mindedly as the sun rose higher in the sky and beat down relentlessly on the ant heap of humanity below.

The majority of pickers lived in the shantytown dwellings that ringed the dump. Eddie was lucky that he was only there on the weekends and could go home to a nice house with his own room and clean water at the end of the day. The residents got their water from a couple of heavily polluted streams that ran through the site. Eddie brought his own water in a plastic bottle from which he sipped sparingly through the course of the day. He also had a couple of bananas to take the edge off his hunger until he could get home. Sometimes he looked longingly at the stalls selling small plates of meat and rice until he reminded himself that the meat on offer had come from the garbage bags of restaurants or hotels. The scraps were fried in oil in hopes of killing off bacteria. Only a couple of pesos a plate, but he needed to work all day to make sixty. Each weekend, he would hand over a hundred pesos to his aunt.

His parents were making enormous sacrifices to get him a good education, and he was the only one of their nine children who would get this opportunity. The family's hopes rested on his doing well and getting a decent-paying job. Then maybe he could pay for one or two of his younger siblings. Picking was a solitary occupation, for all the mass of humanity teeming around him. He was a part-timer and not part of the shanty community. There was one young girl, Corazon, who he teamed up with from time to time whenever they worked in the same part of the dump. She was a precious metal picker, and Smokey Mountain was all she knew. They found it more efficient to scavenge together, each one sharing with the other the metal they found that was not their stock in trade.

The trucks came in an endless stream, hour after interminable hour. There was a rhythm to the work. Push your way to the front to get the choicest morsels. Help tear open the garbage bags and quickly sift through them before the bulldozer moved in to clear the ground for the next truckload. Eddie could tell the time by the sun's position in the sky and the bells of the nearby churches tolling the hour.

Corazon was not there today, and he was disappointed. It wasn't because he thought her attractive. She wasn't. It meant that he would have no civil conversation all day. Certainly, there was a lot of cursing and "what are you doing on my patch, kid?" But Eddie was tall and strong for his age and better nourished than most of the surrounding men. He learned that he just had to stand his ground, and most of the time nothing came of the threats. He had suffered a bad beating early on at his time at the dump. His aunt wanted to forbid him from going there again, but his uncle said he would just have to learn to stick up for himself. Eddie bought himself a penknife which he always carried with him now. He had never had to use it, but it gave him a sense of security.

At last, the Angelus bells rang out. Eddie made his way over to one of the scrap metal dealers and had his last bag of the day weighed. The dealer paid him 20 pesos. He would re-sell the scrap for twice that. Eddie was weary, but upbeat. Today was a good day. He had cleared 70 pesos. Maybe he would treat himself to an ice cream later. He hurried off to catch his bus.

At the same time Eddie Cruz was leaving for work, Lou Holt's driver was picking Josh up for an outing to Lake Taal. Lou had invited Josh to join him and his girlfriend on a day trip out of the city, and he wanted an early start to beat traffic. Josh had asked Rita to join him the night before, but she declined. She said she would feel too self-conscious and under Lou's scrutiny. Josh was irritated by the refusal. He didn't understand how she could hang out with all sorts of characters at Mogombo yet baulk at a small boating party.

They had argued about it.

"If you insist I go, Joshua, then I will. You're paying for my time after all," Rita pouted.

"For Chrissake, Rita, that's not what I want, and you know it. I just think it would be nice to get out of the city with some friends, that's all."

"They're your friends, not mine."

"Have it your own way, Rita, I'm not going to force you."

They had turned their backs on each other in the bed. When Joshua woke, however, he found Rita curled up beside him, her head resting on his chest. Gently, he eased himself out so as not to wake her. She looked so young and vulnerable in sleep. He gazed at her fondly for a few seconds and then quietly got ready to leave.

The trip to Lake Taal, thirty miles south, took a couple of hours. Even that early on a Saturday morning, it took the best part of an hour just to get to the outskirts of Manila. Josh rode up front with the driver. Lou and his girlfriend, Marta, were in the back. There was not much conversation, and the day-trippers spent much of the time dozing. Occasionally, Josh opened his eyes to see the dense, ramshackle dwellings on the city's edges give way to green, unspoiled countryside. It was still early when the driver reached Tagaytay, the tourist town that overlooked the lake.

Marta came to life. "I'm hungry, Lou."

"We can likely grab a sandwich from one of the vendors before we get on the boat, Marta." Lou was keen to go snorkelling.

"I don't want a sandwich; I want a cooked breakfast," Marta insisted.

"Do you now?" Lou was put out. "You *are* packing on the pounds, honey, with that appetite of yours. Keep it up and I'll be in the market for your younger, slimmer replacement, sweet cheeks."

Marta became sullen. One look at her pouting face was enough to convince Lou that if he wanted to avoid a poisonous atmosphere all day it would be best to relent.

"Oh, have it your way. We'll pull over once we hit the main drag and find a café or something."

For someone who was not keen on a sit-down meal, Lou did full justice to the breakfast. He powered his way through eggs, bacon, and pancakes as Marta tucked into a tapsilog with copious amounts of rice. Josh contented himself with fresh pandesal and coffee.

The temperature was already well into the 80s by the time they got on the banka boat Lou had hired for the day. There was a breeze off the lake that moderated the humidity. The banka, a traditional craft of the Philippines, was an outrigger canoe with an engine. A canopy in the middle of the deck provided shade from the blistering sun. Marta curled up like a cat under the canopy while Lou and Josh spent the first couple of hours snorkelling.

There was a whiff of sulphur in the water. The lake was, after all, situated in the caldera of a volcano. After a while the sulphur made Josh feel nauseous, so he retreated to the boat and stretched out to sunbathe.

He was relieved in a way that Lou continued to snorkel. A sort of tension had arisen between Lou and him since he began seeing Rita. Mogombo was Lou's favourite hangout, and because of Rita, Josh did not like to spend time there anymore. It would mean having to look at other men pawing her. His routine was to wait outside each night for the end of her shift, and then walk her home. He liked to spend a couple of hours with her when they got back to the apartment. Since most nights it was after midnight before she finished, he had taken to napping for a couple of hours in the evening. It was the only way he could be fit for work the next day. The change in his routine irked Lou, who preferred to keep him as a drinking buddy. Josh had cheerfully assented to this day trip as a way of making amends.

It's probably better Rita is not with us, Josh thought. *Her presence would probably only aggravate Lou.*

There was a cooler on board with beer, water, and sandwiches, but Josh was content to stick with water. Drinking beer in this tropical heat would only give him a headache. Lou, on the other hand, polished off three large cans as soon as he finished his time in the water.

The captain anchored the boat in a spot he claimed was good for fishing and Josh and Lou put lines out to catch maliputo, which were plentiful in the lake. Josh noted the captain had skeins of his own over the side and was landing a decent number of sardinella for himself while Josh and Lou's rods stayed stubbornly slack.

Marta took no interest in the proceedings, alternately leafing through a couple of magazines she brought or dozing in the sun. She made monosyllabic answers when Lou tried to engage her in conversation. As the afternoon wore on, Lou's mood grew sour, and he began to rib Josh about his relationship with Rita.

"So how's the great romance going then, Romeo?"

"I wouldn't call it that, Lou." Josh glanced back at Marta, but she did not appear to be listening.

"What else would you call it, sport? You hanging around every night to walk your lady love home after her hard day's work giving blowjobs in the back of Mogombo."

"Cut it out, Lou. Rita is not like that." Josh's face flushed bright red, and his knuckles clenched.

"Come off it, Josh. The girl has fed you a line and you've fallen for it. She's just an innocent country mouse trying to make a living in the big, bad city. She's going to quit her line of work as soon as she puts a little bit by for herself and her poor, aged parents." He sneered. "Horseshit! She probably has a brood of brats and a layabout husband back in whatever podunk village she comes from, which she's conveniently forgotten to tell you about. All these girls have a story to pull at the heartstrings. They're just looking for some gullible sap like you, buddy, to fall for it."

Josh leapt to his feet, enraged, and instantly regretted it.

Lou was in his face a split second later, aggressive and belligerent. "You think you can take me, sunshine? Let's just see you try."

The boat rocked with their movement and the startled captain let loose a torrent of Tagalog.

Lou's face was flushed, his hands clenching and unclenching convulsively. Josh looked around desperately for something to defend himself with, as the man in front of him seemed ready to beat him to a pulp. As if from nowhere, Marta interposed herself between the two of them.

She pressed herself against Lou and placed her hands firmly on his shoulders. "You're going to capsize the boat, Lou. I can't swim. You've had too much sun and too many beers. Arguing like this is just spoiling our day out. Sit down and I'll massage your neck and shoulders."

The colour began to recede from Lou's face. He put his arms round Marta's waist. As quickly as it had arisen, the angry mood left. He had morphed from a human wrecking ball to a disoriented bear and sat back down on the side of the boat. Marta, ignoring Josh, positioned herself close behind him and started to massage his temples and neck with expert fingers before turning her attention to his upper back.

Josh drifted in the direction of the captain who was busy hauling in his nets. He was at a loss for what to do or say. Several minutes passed in awkward silence.

"You done with fishing, Steinberg?" Lou called out over his shoulder.

"Pretty much, Lou."

"Let's head back in. Ramon, call it quits. I'll pay you for the whole day of course."

"We can split the cost if you like," Josh offered.

"No need." Lou's voice was curt.

The ride back to the shore seemed to take forever. There was no further conversation on the boat. Josh replayed in his head over and over what Lou had said about Rita. Waves of anger and resentment continued to sweep over him. He could not brush the assertions off, because they had a smell of truth about them. That was why Lou had infuriated him. Everything he knew about Rita was only what she had told him. She might indeed have a husband and children in the provinces. How was he to know? She could well be a consummate liar.

Lou's driver was waiting for them when they docked and Lou had reverted to his usually cheery self. "Might as well head back. Beat the evening rush."

"You and Marta go on. I'll catch a local cab in a bit." Josh was in no mood to share a ride back to the city with him.

"Suit yourself." Lou shrugged and, with an arm around Marta, strolled off toward his car.

For Josh, the ride back was a stark contrast to the luxury of Lou's air-conditioned limousine that morning. He was in a beaten-up sedan with no suspension, and seatbelts that didn't work. His driver might have been anywhere from forty to sixty, with crooked teeth stained from chewing tobacco. He continually leaned out his window as they drove to expel a stream of yellow spittle, but Josh could hardly complain. The trip was only costing him a thousand pesos. It would doubtless have been cheaper if he had bothered to haggle more but he was out of sorts and his attempt at bargaining was half-hearted.

All the way back he brooded on what Lou had said. Was he deluding himself that Rita had feelings for him? Was she indeed just using him as a meal ticket? He was determined to get a straight answer out of her.

Because Lou had cut the trip short, he was home several hours earlier than anticipated. Rita was not at the apartment. Josh banged his fists on the table in frustration. Where the hell was she?

She's likely gone to work early. The thought calmed him somewhat.

Chapter Ten

Philip Wentworth was in a rut. As he sat restlessly in first class on the last leg of his journey from London to Manila, he considered how to spice up his stay there. The BA flight from Heathrow to Hong Kong had been a nightmare. He caught the later of the two daily direct flights, not realising they were designated non-smoking and smoking. Twelve hours of sitting in a fog of cigarette smoke had left him with a splitting headache and his suit reeked of tobacco. Fortunately, he spent a day in Hong Kong so he could have his tailor there measure him for two new ones. The man worked through the night to have them ready before he returned to the airport and he left his old suit hanging in the hotel closet. It had cost him six hundred pounds from Saville Row but he could just write it off against his travel expenses.

This latest trip to Manila was not strictly necessary, of course. He could just as easily have conducted the business over the phone. However, a week at home with his wife Penny in St. Albans was as much as he could stick. She had badgered him to attend the Christmas Concert at Winchester where his two sons were being educated for obscene amounts of money. The only saving grace was that they were boarders, so he didn't see very much of them.

Normally he could escape Penny and her endless chatter about the neighbours and the goings-on of the local hunt, of which she was an enthusiastic member, by staying at his club in London for a couple of nights. When he suggested the idea this time, though, she insisted on joining him.

"I'll go with you, Philip. I want to shop for Christmas presents and I need a new outfit for the hunt ball. We can stay at Claridge's. The Royal Ballet is performing Sleeping Beauty. I'm sure I can get a box. It will be fun."

The bloody woman went through money like water. The vet bill for her horse in the month of November alone was over a thousand. There always seemed to be something wrong with the wretched animal, and that wasn't even considering the cost of stabling the brute. Philip felt compelled to manufacture a crisis in the Philippines that required his immediate attention.

He mulled over how he was going to alter the arrangements for his stay. For a start, he would hire a car and drive himself. Traffic in Manila was chaotic, but no worse than London. It would keep him sharp. He would book at the Manila Hotel for a change of scene. He probably should have been staying there anyway. It was a favourite haunt of the wealthy local families, and he stood a better chance of making useful connections there. He only used the Peninsula for its proximity to the business district and the company offices.

Wentworth toyed with the idea of exchanging Angel for a new girl, but decided against it. He was used to her and she knew what he liked in bed. Most importantly, she didn't bother him about her family like others of her ilk. You no sooner slept with some Filipinas and they started bleating on about some relation of theirs in the UK or Hong Kong or some Arab country that needed this or that favour and could he help out. As if he didn't pay them enough for their services.

It was late Friday evening when he landed in Manila. The cover story for Penny was that he needed the weekend to recover from jet lag before starting work. Pure fiction, of course, but it seemed to wash with her. He decided to spend the night at the Peninsula and swap over to the Manila Hotel the next day.

After a leisurely breakfast the following morning, Wentworth drove in his rented Mercedes convertible down to the bay. He enjoyed weaving his way through the city traffic and startling pedestrians trying to cross the thoroughfares by blaring on the horn. He was very impressed with the ambience of the fabled Manila Hotel. It was reminiscent of colonial elegance and service. The staff was courteous, efficient, and knew their place. There was none of this banter, as if they were your social equal.

This place would give Raffles in Singapore a run for its money, he thought.

He phoned Angel and told her to meet him at the Manila Jockey Club. The afternoon was spent very pleasantly at the track, and he managed to back three winners. They dined at a new sushi restaurant near the water. The trouble started when Wentworth returned to his hotel and tried to take Angel up to his room. A security man at the bank of elevators firmly blocked their access.

"I'm sorry, sir. This young woman cannot accompany you upstairs."

"What the fuck are you talking about?" Wentworth was belligerent. He had been drinking all afternoon, had wine at dinner, and finished up with a couple of large brandies in the lobby before deciding to call it a night.

"The policy of the hotel is that lady *companions*—" The man looked significantly at Angel. "—are not allowed in the guest rooms."

"That's fucking horse shit. I want to speak to the manager, you prick."

The guard ignored the insult. "If you inquire at the desk, sir, I'm sure they will be able to arrange that for you."

"You." Wentworth turned to Angel and pointed out a chair in the lobby. "Sit over there until I've sorted these clowns out."

The manager, summoned, took the Englishman to his office. Wentworth, his face red and breathing heavily, rummaged in his wallet, took out a credit card, and slammed it down on the desk.

"I don't know what kind of dump you're running here, but you know what this is? It's a Coutts Card backed by Coutts of London. I could take the most expensive suite in this shit hole for a year with this card. So, what sort of room do I need to buy here so I can have my friend stay over with no more complaints?"

"That would be the McArthur Suite, sir, where the general stayed, but it makes no difference to our policy. We have certain standards of behaviour that we expect our guests to observe."

"You're a jumped-up boarding house in a Third World excuse for a country. Where do you get off spouting on about standards, you supercilious asswipe?" Wentworth, who had been yelling, suddenly switched to a clipped British accent of total disdain. "Be good enough to have my car brought round and send my things over to the Peninsula."

He lumbered to his feet and made his way slowly, if a little unsteadily, to the door.

The hotel manager sat rigid in his chair from the effort to control himself. "I think your decision to change lodging is by far the best solution, Mr Wentworth."

"Don't even think about sending me a bill for this cesspit," was Wentworth's parting shot. The manager, already on the phone with the valet desk, ignored him.

Eddie Cruz hummed happily to himself as he walked quickly home along a tree-lined street near his uncle and aunt's house. He was returning from the ice cream parlour where he hung out with his friends. A hurried sandwich in the kitchen and a quick shower and change of clothes from his day at the dump had bought him this couple of hours of carefree escape.

Eddie was listening to a New Kids on the Block cassette on his Walkman, hooked on the belt of his jeans, headset tucked under his baseball cap. He had swapped his Bon Jovi album for it with another kid. The cassettes were all knockoffs, and the quality wasn't great, but no one cared. It was a cheap form of entertainment. The others had stuck around at the outdoor café, and there was one cute girl who really seemed into him, but he was back at Smokey Mountain tomorrow and there was Sunday Mass to attend, so he had taken off. Half dancing to the music, he turned onto the side street that led to the back entrance of their house.

Angel was impassive when Philip Wentworth came back.

"We're leaving," was all he said.

She took secret pleasure in his obvious discomfort. The Manila Hotel was known for its no-call-girl policy. Better men than Philip Wentworth had tried and failed to smuggle their paramours into its bedrooms, some coming up with the most ingenious subterfuges. It was a point of pride among the hotel staff to identify and eject the young women who plied their trade among its wealthy patrons. When he sobered up and had time to think about it, he would blame her for not warning him. She planned to play to his ego by swearing she thought he had the influence to pull it off. What did alarm her, as they stood at the valet desk on the steps of the hotel, was the realisation that he intended to drive.

"Are you not jet-lagged and tired, Philip my love? Would it not be better to take a limousine?" She knew better than to suggest he had had too much to drink. He would only fly into a rage.

The Mercedes pulled up. "I'm perfectly fine. Just get in the damn car."

Without bothering to tip the parking attendant, he put the powerful automobile in gear and, revving the engine, raced out toward Roxas Boulevard. Angel was terrified. Wentworth had driven aggressively earlier in the day. Now he was manic.

He weaved in and out of traffic, barely missing other cars, sending pedestrians flying in all directions to avoid him, cursing volubly at anyone or anything that got in his way. It was Saturday night and traffic was even heavier than usual. Stopped at an intersection for over ten minutes by a disabled garbage truck, Wentworth flew into a paroxysm of rage. He hit the horn with his fist and kept it there, screaming obscenities which were fully audible as they sat stationary in the top-down convertible. Angel cringed in embarrassment. She made herself as small as she could, shrinking into the leather upholstery, arms tightly by her side, head down on her chest.

"Fuck it all to hell. We'll take the side streets." Spying a turnoff just ahead of them, Wentworth ran the car onto the sidewalk. An elderly woman screamed in fright as his wing mirror struck her with a glancing blow. Wentworth ignored the cry as he jerked the wheel and sped up the narrow lane.

"If we just keep going east, we'll hit Makati," he said loudly, shifting up and down through the gears.

Angel felt the taste of bile in her mouth.

"Almost there," Wentworth grunted. He shifted down abruptly and turned into yet another side street. In a matter of seconds, he had transitioned from first gear to fourth, the powerful car hurtling forward.

Neither of them saw the young man silhouetted against the wall of the alley until it was too late.

Eddie Cruz took the entire force of the Mercedes. It struck him full on, sending him over the bonnet to smash headfirst into the wall of a building. Wentworth hit the brakes. Dazed, Angel turned around to look back. The boy lay broken and lifeless on the road behind them, his face horribly disfigured.

Angel cried out in anguish. "Philip, what have you done?"

Chapter Eleven

Bongo Cruz was seated at a typewriter in his bedroom when he heard frantic pounding on the front door. At first, he ignored it. He was finishing his latest report on the security strengths and weaknesses of Fort Bonifacio.

He bought the typewriter from a local second-hand market and planned to get rid of it before the coup to cover his tracks. This was the fourth such report he had generated in just over a week and was meticulous and detailed like the rest.

The pattern it established was that while the fort was a formidable defensive asset when adequately manned, the current arrangements were pretty lax. At first, all he described was the daily movement of personnel and goods in and out of the fort. As he progressed in his surveillance, however, he documented the exact number of guards at each entry point, how they were armed, and how often and when they were relieved. He took careful note of how the guard posts communicated with the barracks located in the middle of the fort complex. By loitering unobtrusively in the administration building's doorway, he was able to observe a routine security drill. This allowed him to time how long it took for troops in the barracks to be scrambled to the guard posts. The nature of his job meant he had no problem inventorying exactly what weaponry was stored in the armoury, and therefore potentially available to the fort's defenders.

The more information he assembled, the more Bongo found himself warming to the task, almost in spite of himself. The challenge was to take the fort without provoking a bloodbath. For now, his only contact with the coup plotters was Andres Soledad. As he began to formulate a detailed plan on how to best seize the fort, he resolved to move up the chain of command. *I'm not having that prick take credit for my work,* he thought. *I mean to be well rewarded for the risks I'm taking.*

"Get down here, Bongo!" His father had to roar to make himself heard above the wails of anguish coming from his mother. Startled, Bongo took the stairs two at a time.

"Eddie's dead." His father was ashen. He was cradling his wife in his arms, as anguished sobs shook her tiny frame.

"He's been run over by a car just down the street. Our next-door neighbour Joseph saw it happen. He just told us. Go over there now. I'll join you as soon as I can. Your mother can't be left on her own."

Bongo felt the familiar rush of adrenaline he experienced when in a combat situation. "Which direction, left or right?" he asked curtly.

"It's in the alley that joins our street. Bottom of the road on the right."

Bongo set out at a sprint.

When he arrived at the scene, Bongo observed the salient details with professional detachment. There was a lot of blood. Eddie's head was crushed. He was completely disfigured. The middle-aged man, who he took to be the driver, was perched on the boot of a late-model Mercedes convertible. There was a girl, looking distraught, squatting against the alley wall some little distance from where Eddie lay. A few onlookers shook their heads, murmuring among themselves at the entrance to the alley from the main road which ran parallel to their street. He could hear the sound of police sirens drawing closer.

Bongo was not particularly affected by the sight of his dead cousin. He just associated Eddie with a persistent smell of rotting garbage. It was hard luck the little shit had got himself run over, but at least he wouldn't be stinking up the house anymore. Bongo made a beeline for the girl. On his way over to her, however, he made sure to pass close by Philip Wentworth.

"You okay, sir? You're not hurt?"

Wentworth looked at him with a dazed expression. "I'm fine. Just a bit shook up is all."

Bongo registered the strong smell of alcohol on Wentworth's breath before kneeling down beside Angel. "Hi there. I'm Bongo, Bongo Cruz. I'm the kid's cousin. You with the guy that was driving?" he said in Tagalog.

Angel nodded dumbly.

Bongo leaned in and spoke in a low confidential whisper. "Who is he exactly?"

Angel met his gaze. Bongo could see she was in shock. Well, the medics could deal with that when they got there. Right now, he needed information before the cops arrived. He willed himself to smile gently at her and took one of her hands in his. "It's been a big shock, I know. What's your name, honey?"

"Angel." She was shivering.

He put a comforting arm around her. "There'll be some medics here shortly, Angel. You'll be okay. But I need to know. Who is the guy that was driving the car?"

Mechanically, she told him.

"So let me get this straight. He's a British businessman who spends a fair amount of time over here, and you are his companion while he's in town." He used the euphemism for the relationship with practised skill. Angel nodded. Bongo had the information he needed.

He called over to an older woman who was standing off to the side praying. "This young girl is in shock. Can you stay with her until the ambulance comes?" He spoke in a calm, authoritative voice. It was a voice that expected to be obeyed.

The woman, initially startled to be addressed so directly, met his eye, and after a moment's hesitation moved to join them. Having successfully handed off the role of Angel's comforter, Bongo turned his attention to Wentworth. He walked quickly over to the car and sat on the bonnet beside him. Wentworth was chalk white and visibly shaking. His breathing was rapid and shallow. There was spittle on his chin.

"Mr Wentworth, how are you holding up, sir? You seem to be in shock. It was a terrible accident. Try to take a few deep breaths. Help is on the way."

Philip Wentworth gazed dumbly at the young Filipino beside him.

"My name is Bongo Cruz, sir. I'm the cousin of the kid you hit, Eddie Cruz. He never had much road sense, poor Eddie. He grew up in a small village. His parents sent him here to Manila for his education. He was the brightest one in the family. They had such high hopes for him. It will be a devastating blow to them."

As Bongo was speaking, he slid off the bonnet and rose to his feet, forcing Wentworth to look up at him as he delivered this information.

"The boy is dead?" Wentworth was stunned.

"I'm afraid so, yes. Instantaneous I should say. I'm in the military. I see a lot of death, unfortunately." Bongo was matter-of-fact.

There was an approaching sound of sirens.

"As it's a fatality, the police are going to be asking a lot of questions, Mr Wentworth," Bongo continued. "They'll be here any minute now. Dealing with them can be a bit overwhelming if you're not a local, particularly for something as serious as this. I can have a word with them if you like. Explain about Eddie. Make the identification and so on."

"Why would you help me like this?" Wentworth was confused.

"It's a tragic accident, and I don't see the point of having this become confrontational. It won't bring the boy back. If the family don't kick up a stink the police will likely accept it as an accident, with a bit of persuasion, if you understand what I'm saying."

Wentworth's eyes narrowed as comprehension dawned.

Got him, Bongo thought triumphantly. He took care to remain impassive.

Wentworth heaved himself off the bonnet of the car and, conscious of the approaching sirens, attempted to straighten his appearance.

"I quite agree with you, Bongo, is it?" Bongo acknowledged the use of his name with a quick nod. "I offer my sincere condolences to you and your family on this tragic loss. I'm sure there will be financial repercussions from the boy's death. I feel I ought to help out in some way…" Wentworth's voice trailed off.

"I'm going to need to break the news to his parents," Bongo said. "Once they get over the shock, I'm sure they will be grateful for that kind offer, Mr Wentworth."

Looking over Wentworth's shoulder Bongo could see his father running down the alley toward them. He needed to make sure there wasn't going to be a confrontation. "I'll have a word with the police as soon as they arrive. I'll be in touch tomorrow once we've managed to attend to poor Eddie here, Lord grant him peace." Bongo crossed himself piously.

"I'm staying at the Peninsula Hotel," Wentworth blurted out.

"Don't worry, I'll find you."

Bongo was already moving in the direction of his father, who was staring down in horror at his nephew's broken body. Someone had draped a light rain jacket over the boy's face for decorum's sake, but the twisted position of the limbs left no doubt as to the violence of the impact.

"Who did this to him?" His father's voice was hoarse, a mixture of grief and anger.

"That clown over there." Bongo jerked his head in the direction of Philip Wentworth. The older man began to move as if he intended to confront the perpetrator.

"No, Tatay!" Bongo said sharply. "I've talked to the guy. He's a wealthy Brit. He's prepared to offer compensation."

"Compensation. What are you talking about, compensation? The bastard ran Eddie over. There needs to be justice for the boy."

Bongo's father tried to get past him and Bongo grabbed him by the shoulders. "Justice is a luxury for those who can afford it, Tatay. Eddie is dead. His parents and sisters are not. This guy will pay plenty to stay out of trouble. If we act sensibly, it means a better life for Eddie's whole family. Think what the boy would want if it were up to him."

His father made as if to break free, but just as suddenly his body went limp. He seemed to shrink into himself. "I always suspected you were callous, Bongo. Until now I never understood how brutal you really are."

"We should save the recriminations for another day, Tatay. Right now, I need you to stay with Eddie. Make sure the kid is treated with proper respect. I'm going to make sure the guys investigating this don't throw a spanner in the works. After that, I'll track down his sister, Rita. She should probably be the one to break the news to their parents."

A police car pulled up and Bongo headed in the direction of the approaching officers.

Chapter Twelve

As Bongo drove to Mogombo to track down Rita, he considered how much Philip Wentworth could be shaken down for. He also gave some thought as to whether he should pay himself a commission for brokering a deal. He'd put the bite on Wentworth for 75,000 sterling, and when the bastard baulked—as he surely would—they'd settle for 55,000. That would be 50,000 for the family and 5,000 to bribe the investigating officers. He decided to leave himself out of it. *Blood is thicker than water at the end of the day.*

Besides, there were other ways he could make money. Rita would go along with it once she stopped having hysterics over the kid's death. He'd leave her no choice. It would be do as he said, or he'd tell her parents she was a sex worker. Bongo regarded having to deal with the fallout from Eddie's death as an unwelcome distraction. He took it on out of a grudging sense of family loyalty, and he was not one to second guess himself once he had decided on a course of action.

Satisfied with his plan, Bongo returned to the problem of what role he should play in the plot to overthrow Corazon Aquino. This was where real money could be made. If Imelda Marcos was financing the effort, opportunity abounded. Bongo had already demonstrated his value to the plotters with his intelligence reports on Fort Bonifacio. He now had a plan of attack against the fort, which exploited the security weaknesses he'd identified and came with a starring role for himself. Nothing too dangerous, of course, but if he could get up the chain of command, Bongo was confident he could extract a tidy sum in exchange for his expertise.

Play this right and I can write my own ticket; I'll be made for life.

Bongo's eyes gleamed as he pulled up in front of Mogombo. The place was hopping. In the space just in front of the jukebox a burly shirtless man was spinning around and around with one of the bar girls stretched across his shoulders, clinging to him like a limpet as a group of guys cheered him on. The other bar girls were yelling at the young Filipina to hang on tight. *A game of strip poker gone out of hand.*

He looked around for Rita, finding her in the corner, perched on the lap of a bald, middle-aged guy. She looked at him anxiously as he approached, her eyes darting to the ever-watchful mama-san.

Bongo adopted the menacing air he used to employ to intimidate civilians. "Show's over, friend. Time you got yourself a new playmate. I need a word with my cousin here."

"Fuck off, wetback. I paid good money for this piece of ass," the man said in an American accent.

Without compunction, Bongo delivered a karate chop to the man's throat, causing him to snort in pain and jerk backwards, gasping for air. Rita fell to the floor in front of him.

"Get up," Bongo said. "We're leaving. Your brother Eddie is dead. Got himself run over by a car." He pulled her to her feet, and with his arm around her waist, half-dragged, half-carried her toward the door before the bouncers had time to react.

As they neared an older woman who was watching them wide-eyed, he said, "Sorry, Mama-san, family emergency. Bar fine the girl for the asshole I punched. This should cover it."

Bongo pulled out a wad of pesos and threw them on a nearby table. The mama-san's practised eye quickly calculated the amount. The sharp crack of her folded fan on the counter and a shake of her head forestalled the bouncers.

Rita sat slumped in the passenger seat of Bongo's Land Rover, shaking uncontrollably. The incomprehensible news of her brother's death and the violent manner of her departure from the bar created a tumult of emotion. Feelings of disbelief, grief, and helplessness competed for dominance.

Bongo drummed his fingers impatiently on the steering wheel. "Pull yourself together, Rita. There's a lot to do. You can't see my parents dressed like that."

"I don't understand, Bongo." Rita could barely get the words out, her voice a whisper.

"What is there to understand, Rita? Your brother got himself run over. It happens a lot in this town."

"I have the street clothes I came in. I'll go in the back way and get them," she said in a lifeless voice.

"Hurry up about it. And don't make me have to go back in there and get you," Bongo said with an edge.

The journey back to Bongo's parents' house was mostly silent. Bongo pre-empted Rita's questions by summarising the salient facts surrounding Eddie's death. He was surprised to get no pushback from Rita when he detailed his plan to extract payment from Philip Wentworth in exchange for covering up the vehicular homicide. Rita, with the bitter experience of a year living in Manila, and the difficulty of making enough to send money home, was forced to accept the cruel logic of what Bongo proposed.

The events of the rest of the night had a nightmarish quality. Her aunt was inconsolable. "I told the boy it was dangerous to go out working on the refuse dump. How am I going to face my sister-in-law? She trusted me with him."

There was stunned silence at the end of the phone as Rita broke the news to her mother, followed by a scream of anguish. The subsequent conversation with her father was more subdued, as he fretted about how soon Eddie could be brought home for burial, and how they would be able to pay for it. There was her feeling of disgust at how quickly her father latched on to Bongo's assertion that the driver of the vehicle could be persuaded to pay compensation.

"How much does Bongo think he'll be willing to pay? How soon would we get the money? Is Bongo with you now? Put him on the phone."

How could she blame the man? Eddie was one of nine children. There were still eight others for him to worry about. Bongo had pulled some strings. There would be a quick autopsy report and Eddie's body would be released within forty-eight hours.

Josh was waiting up for her at the apartment when she got back. There was a half empty bottle of whiskey on the table in front of him.

"So, Rita. Did you have a good time with your new boyfriend? There's no point in lying to me. I phoned the bar. One of the girls told me you left with a young local guy who came looking for you."

He was aggressive, his voice slightly slurred.

"That was Bongo, my cousin," Rita said wearily. He was so drunk and consumed by jealousy he did not register how distressed she was.

"Your cousin. Yeah, right."

"Bongo came to tell me that my brother Eddie has been killed, run over by another drunken expat businessman like you. Did the girl at the bar tell you that Eddie dragged me out of the place, or did she forget to mention it? I've come back for some clothes. I'm going to need to travel home to my village with his body. I'll move out completely after his funeral if that's what you want." Her voice broke as she was speaking and she started to tremble.

Josh stared at her, his mouth open, and desperately tried to gather his wits. The anger he had been nursing against her evaporated. He was left feeling bewildered and inadequate.

"Jeez, what a fuckwad I am," he said, stumbling to his feet. "I'm really sorry, Rita. I should have known better." He groped for something else to say. "Have you eaten?"

The words sounded trite and Rita shook her head wearily.

"Sit down," he said. "I'll make you something. Tell me exactly what happened."

Rita felt an overwhelming impulse to just grab what few clothes she had in the apartment and leave. She knew it was what she should do. But she felt so exhausted and drained. She allowed him to push her into the wooden chair and sat there looking at him blankly as he rummaged around in the fridge.

He presented her with a slapdash ham sandwich and a glass of milk. As an afterthought, he grabbed an apple from the fruit bowl on the counter and placed it beside the plate with the sandwich. Listlessly, she began to eat.

"When will you leave for the provinces?" Josh asked. "I should come with you."

Rita sat bolt upright and looked at Josh incredulously. "Are you mad? It's either that or you're being exceptionally stupid. It's out of the question."

"I don't understand." He was bewildered. "Couldn't you simply say I was a friend?"

"Young Filipino girls of good family do not just arrive with boyfriends in tow, particularly foreign ones, Joshua. People would draw the obvious conclusion about our relationship. My parents would be publicly humiliated." She sighed and wearily brushed the hair out of her eyes.

Josh nodded his head in reluctant agreement. "You're right, of course, I wasn't thinking." They were silent for a time as he leaned against the kitchen counter while Rita sat at the table with her face in her hands. After a while, he said, "I can at least pay for the cost of taking your brother home for burial."

Rita was astonished. "Why would you want to do that?"

"Because I love you," he said simply.

The sad little cortege left early the next morning. A cab dropped Josh and Rita off near the morgue, and the two of them waited a discreet distance away for the others to arrive. After a short while standing quietly side by side, they watched Bongo give the waiting hearse driver instructions before ushering Rita's aunt and uncle inside.

Despite the heat, Rita was dressed in a black frock. "I'd best go. Bongo doesn't like to be kept waiting."

"When will you be back?" Josh felt very protective of her looking so fragile and forlorn.

"In a week I suppose," she said, resigned.

"That's a long time just to bury someone."

"There has to be the lamay, the wake, before the actual service. I think my father is planning for it to last five nights. Just the thought of it makes me feel anxious."

Josh hugged her shoulders. "I don't know why I imagined it would be shorter. We had to sit shiva for my aunt for a week after she died. The only difference is the sequencing. Jews bury them first and the mourning period comes after." He gave her an envelope stuffed with peso notes. "Here, take this. It will help with the expenses. I'm sorry for your poor brother's loss, Rita, I truly am."

She took the money gratefully, looked around, and gave him a quick kiss. "I'll call to let you know when I'm coming back home."

Joshua felt an irrational surge of pleasure at the phrase. Rita ran briskly across the street and into the austere building. He hung around to watch the party leave. The coffin was wheeled out on a gurney and loaded into the hearse without ceremony. As the two cars pulled away, Josh could not help feeling sad for the young boy he had never met.

Chapter Thirteen

Philip Wentworth woke with a start. He was not sure where he was, and it took a few seconds for his eyes to adjust to the darkness. Gradually, he recognised the hotel room of the Peninsula. Angel was asleep in the bed beside him. He looked at the alarm clock. It was 8:30 a.m. The heavy curtains on the windows completely blocked out the brilliant morning sunshine. He propped himself up on the pillows and turned on the bedside light, surveying the room resentfully.

He felt trapped. He was supposed to be back in England. Three days after the accident, the police had impounded his passport. Just a few formalities to cover and the unfortunate affair would be put to bed. That was the official line. The reality was, as Bongo Cruz had succinctly explained, he needed to come up with fifty-five thousand pounds. That was what it would take to pay off the family and bribe the officials. Until he forked over the money, he was going nowhere, and he might find himself in considerable legal jeopardy if he came up short.

Wentworth cursed the Manila Hotel for its stuck-up Victorian attitude. If it weren't for them, he would never have been driving in the first place. He cursed the stupid kid for running out on the road like that.

The money, that was another thing. It was on its way from his UK Bank. He'd had to withdraw it from the joint account he shared with his wife, Penelope. She didn't often check their bank statements, but it was inevitable she would find out eventually, and he was already racking his brains for a plausible explanation.

Angel stirred beside him, and he looked at her suspiciously. She had seen everything, and she knew how drunk he'd been. Could he trust her to keep her mouth shut?

He swung his feet out to the floor feeling for the hotel slippers. Grunting heavily, he lumbered to the bathroom. He didn't bother to raise the seat. Urine splashed all around the toilet. Grabbing the dressing gown from the back of the door he put it on and went to the telephone to dial for room service.

"I'll have my usual, bacon, scrambled eggs, mushrooms, brown toast, fresh orange juice, and coffee. Make that for two," he added, as an afterthought, glancing at his still sleeping companion.

Wentworth hung up and pulled the curtains back. "Wake up, Angel, breakfast will be here shortly. Go make yourself respectable. I don't want the attendant to find you lying in bed."

Angel stirred grudgingly.

"Well, what are you waiting for girl? You heard what I said."

She did as she was bid, thinking all the while how ridiculous the pretence of respectability was. The hotel staff knew exactly what was going on. Her sitting demurely on the sofa in the living room area of the suite was fooling no one. As she dried her hair in the bathroom, Angel vowed that she would finish with Wentworth. She despised him. His callous indifference toward the victim of his drunken rampage had revealed the depth of his depravity. She would find herself another patron, and as soon as she did, she would disappear out of his life. She just needed an excuse so she would not have to see him for a couple of days.

Simple, she thought. *I'll just tell him I've started my period.* Wentworth was squeamish about a woman's bodily functions.

He scowled at her as she exited the bathroom. "I hope you kept your mouth shut about my drinking when the police questioned you, Angel."

"We've talked about this already, Philip."

"Tell me again what you said, you dumb bitch. We will damn well talk about anything I want. I'm fucking paying you enough."

Angel answered him, her back turned, as she slipped into her dress. "The police asked me how much alcohol you'd had. I told them you like gin and tonics, but you also drink a lot of water because of the humidity, so I had no idea. I kept repeating that driving in Manila is very confusing if you're not a local. They seemed to buy that."

"Quite the accomplished little liar," Wentworth sneered.

I need to be to tolerate a piece of shit like you, Angel thought.

There was a knock on the door.

"That will be the food. Let the guy in," Wentworth said.

They ate in silence, Angel staring vacantly out the window. Wentworth was preoccupied with his forced detainment in the Philippines and the inevitable confrontation with his wife when she discovered the large withdrawal from their account.

He looked desperately for some other way to extricate himself from his predicament. Maybe if he went to the British embassy and just claimed he had lost his passport. They might issue him with emergency papers. Mulling the idea over in his mind, he inadvertently bit his tongue as he swallowed a piece of toast.

"Fuck!" he exclaimed.

Angel was jerked back from her reverie and looked at him quizzically.

He didn't want to explain the reason for his outburst. It might make him seem ridiculous in her eyes. "Finish up eating. You need to be out of here. I've got things to do."

Instantly she jumped to her feet and reached for her handbag. "I'm not that hungry anyway, Philip. I'll get out of your way. You can phone me when you want to get together next." She couldn't bring herself to kiss him.

She headed for the door, and Wentworth let her go without comment. Who did he know at the embassy? There was that young commercial attaché he had met at a cocktail reception a couple of months back. They had bonded over reminiscences of their time at Oxford. Of course, the guy had gone to Wadham, was a lefty and probably queer, while his college was Christ Church. Wentworth was sorely tempted to give it a go, but then he thought about having to brave the gauntlet at the airport. What if the local police had put something in the system and he was detained? They would throw him in jail. He just didn't have the bottle for it. All he could do was go to the bank once again and see if the wire from Coutts had come through. There was no question of his bank having screwed up the transfer. The problem had to be on the Philippine end.

The visit to the bank accomplished nothing. The manager was unfailingly polite but completely ineffective. Not knowing how else to occupy himself, Wentworth returned to the hotel. When he got to his room, the light on his telephone glowed red with a message from the front desk. A fax had arrived for him from Coutts. Wentworth scowled. It was past 9 p.m. in London.

"When did it come in?" he asked irritably. There was a pause while the desk clerk looked for the timestamp on the fax.

"Two this morning, sir."

"And you're only telling me now?" Wentworth snapped.

"I'm sorry, Mr Wentworth, I'm the day clerk. It was in the machine when I came on duty."

"You Filipino fucks. Nothing is ever your fault."

The insult was ignored. "Would you like me to send the fax to your room sir?"

"Never mind, I'll come down to collect it. Knowing you lot it'll be tonight before it gets delivered."

The fax let informed him that the bank had traced the wire and found an intermediary bank in Hong Kong had transposed a couple of digits when forwarding the funds. This was now rectified and the money would be available to him in three business days. It was Friday. *Fucking hell,* he thought. *It will be Tuesday at the earliest before I lay hands on the money. I need a drink.*

It wasn't even noon, but Wentworth went to the bar and ordered a double whiskey. He sat on a high-backed stool at one end of the counter and thought about his wife. He could already hear the outrage and contempt there would be in her voice if he told her the truth. Maybe he would just tell her he had got a local girl pregnant and the fifty-five thousand was the price of buying her off. Penelope delighted in throwing his sexual inadequacies in his face at every opportunity. She resented the fact that although he had sired two sons, he had been unable to give her the daughter she desperately wanted. The thought of his infidelity and his having a bastard child would infuriate and humiliate her in equal measure. *Would serve the bitch right,* he mused. There was nothing like making lemonade out of lemons. He ordered another whiskey.

Chapter Fourteen

"It's a go!" Bongo Cruz and Andres Soledad were seated at a table in a bar near the Manila fish market. It was noisy and crowded. Workers, coming on or off shift, wearing gum boots and aprons, mingled with tourists taking a break from sightseeing. A slight but pervasive smell of rancid fish hung in the air. Soledad had phoned Bongo a couple of hours earlier and insisted they meet that evening.

"When do we strike?" Bongo felt a rush of adrenaline as he posed the question.

"November 30, a week from today."

Bongo was startled. "That soon?"

"We need to keep the notice short. The longer we leave it the greater the risk of the plan being discovered."

"So, what *is* the plan?" Bongo asked.

Soledad's eyes were darting around constantly, anxious they were not being overheard. He spoke quickly, his voice low and hoarse. "We seize the airports, the TV stations, and secure the port. Corazon Aquino will be captured and detained. We pre-empt a counterstrike by her loyalists by taking out the major military command centres. We'll seize Villamor and Mactan airbases. At the same time, we will overrun Fort Bonifacio. That's where you come in."

Bongo nodded grimly. He was impressed at the scale of the plot now that it was finally unveiled. His gut instinct that the coup was well-financed had proven correct, but his efforts to get closer to the leaders had been only partially successful. There had been a couple of meetings with Gregorio Honasan, one of the key players, and his detailed scheme for how Fort Bonifacio could be secured with a minimum of casualties had been adopted. He had not been able to get Soledad out of the chain of command, however. Still, he had made damned sure that he got the credit for his ideas rather than Soledad.

The core of Bongo's plan was to create a diversion during one of the guard changes at the fort, either morning or evening. He had noticed that the refuse bins around the compound were emptied just once a day, at midday. Placing a small explosive in several of them and detonating them simultaneously would cause confusion and havoc. With the guards distracted and uncertain as to which shift was responsible, it would create an ideal opportunity for the attack.

Bongo had agreed to plant the devices and detonate them. He had dealt enough with C4 plastic explosives back in Mindanao while setting ambushes for the Moro. He had found trip wires to be useless in the jungle, as any kind of animal or villager could stumble into them, so he had learned radio remote control. For the coup, he had fashioned C4 packs and detonators discreetly smuggled from the armoury into small bombs, reshaping the putty to fit into cans.

At the fort, they would be concealed in brown lunch bags that he would casually discard. For the past few weeks, he had made a point of bringing food into the office and eating outside on various benches around the fort complex. He would then casually discard his bag in the nearby refuse bin. No one observing his movements would see anything out of the ordinary while he planted the bombs.

"All the targets will be attacked simultaneously at 7 a.m."

"I'll start planting the devices the evening before," Bongo said.

Soledad needed reassurance. "You're sure there's no chance of them being discovered?"

"None whatsoever. It's a military installation. It's not like you're going to have vagrants rummaging through the trash."

Bongo realised that by being more deeply involved in the plot and getting his hands dirty, he was taking a bigger risk, but the rewards promised to be enormous if the gamble paid off.

I'm on a slow boat to nowhere as things currently stand. A few more years and I'll end up a middle-aged nobody. It's worth a throw of the dice!

"I'll detonate the explosives by remote control at 6:45 a.m. It will cause chaos. The fort garrison should be easy prey after that."

Soledad was mollified. "It's the Rangers, your old regiment, that have been assigned to secure the fort. You're to report to the commander once it's in our hands. He knows we have someone on the inside, but we've not disclosed your identity."

Bongo was quietly relieved. If the plot failed, the fewer people who knew about him the better. "Where will you be when it all kicks off?" he asked.

"At General Zumel's command centre, coordinating intelligence."

Zumel was a Marcos loyalist. He, together with Lt. Colonel Gregorio Honasan, an army strategist, handled the military component of the coup attempt.

Bongo felt nothing but contempt for Soledad's response, but he was careful not to show it. *Gutless weasel has made damn sure he's nowhere near the firing line.*

"For this to be successful, all the targets need to be secured simultaneously. Accurate information must be distilled from the field commanders and communicated clearly to the chain of command." Soledad was almost whining as he tried to justify his role.

"You're just the man for the job, Andres. Best place for you."

Soledad looked at Bongo suspiciously but detected nothing but amiability in his steady gaze. He decided that the undercurrent of sarcasm in the comment was just in his imagination.

Chapter Fifteen

When Josh got into work on Monday morning, he was startled to find that no one was at their terminals. Staff drifted between desks, chatting among themselves. There was a group congregated around the water cooler.

He went over to Lou Holt's station. "What's going on?"

Lou, who was busily plugging numbers into a spreadsheet, looked up from what he was doing. "Hi there, Josh. Come on, I'll show you. You're not going to believe this." He heaved himself out of his chair, grabbed Josh by the elbow, and propelled him toward the door.

"Where are we going?" Josh asked, bewildered.

"To the computer room."

They went down one story into the basement. The computer room was air-conditioned with a front wall of glass. It housed all the paraphernalia of an IBM mainframe installation: consoles, tape and disc drives, and, dwarfing everything, the massive processor itself. There was no one in the room, which struck Josh as unusual. Normally there were at least two systems operators on duty.

The two men surveyed the scene through the glass partition.

"Notice anything unusual?" Lou looked at Josh and grinned.

"Well, there's no one on duty."

"Apart from that?"

Slightly irritated, Josh looked at the room again. "What's that brown liquid leaking from the ceiling?"

"Mrs Steinberg didn't raise any dummies." Lou clapped him on the back. "The brown liquid is shit."

Josh looked at Lou in disbelief. "You can't be serious."

"Serious as a heart attack, old son. Turns out the sewage pipes for the building run through the ceiling above us. One of them sprung a leak. Big Blue here—" Lou waved his arm in the direction of the massive processor. "—swallowed a couple of gallons of excrement before they could plug it. Not, as you can see, entirely successfully. I'll bet this scenario is not in the maintenance handbook for the care and feeding of IBM mainframes."

"So that's why everyone is just standing around," Josh muttered as comprehension dawned.

"Got it in one, sunshine."

"How long are we going to be down?" Josh asked.

"They're flying a couple of guys over from IBM headquarters in New York. Best-case scenario, it'll be a week." Lou shrugged his shoulders resignedly.

"Holy fuck. What will that do to our delivery schedule?"

"I'm working on that right now. We were in the middle of doing a backup when the shit hit the fan, pardon the pun. Also, we don't know if any of the drives have been damaged. It's going to be more than just a week's delay. I can tell you that for nothing."

Josh groaned. "Webster's going to have a conniption. What are the staff going to do in the meantime?"

"With their terminals down there's sod all they can do. Maybe you can have them tidy their desks." Lou shrugged. "At any rate, there's nothing we can do down here. Let's you and me nip out for a coffee and see if we can't come up with a plan of action for the next few days." Lou was already striding for the stairs.

"I'm not sure I can, Lou," Josh said uncertainly. "I'm sure Webster's going to want to talk about all this."

"Not for the next hour he won't." Lou grinned. "He just started a call with IBM. To explain what's happened to their precious mainframe."

They walked out into the brilliant sunshine and parked themselves at a table outside a small coffee shop a few hundred yards from the office. Josh confined himself to a small, iced coffee, but Lou set about demolishing a large fruit Danish, washed down with a cappuccino.

"Need to keep the strength up," he said with his mouth full. He turned serious. "How is the girlfriend holding up?"

Josh took his time to answer, stirring sweetener into his coffee. The crisis at work had diverted his attention for a couple of hours, but now his thoughts returned to the tragedy that had befallen Rita.

"I talked to her last night. Rita's still down with her family. She's planning to come back to Manila with her aunt and uncle tomorrow. She's very upset obviously. Particularly because her cousin Bongo wants to do a deal with the bastard who ran over her kid brother, to have it hushed up for a wad of cash."

Lou sighed. "Life is cheap in this country. People are dirt poor, and they have too many kids. It seems ungodly to strike a bargain like that from our perspective, but her cousin is just being practical."

"It's not right, Lou." Josh slammed the table with his fist. Coffee from his cup spilled all over his pants. "Fuck."

"Whoa, cowboy." Lou grabbed his own drink to stop it from spilling. "I warned you not to get too involved with the locals and their lives, Josh. Always remember, we're just passing through here. These people have their own culture and way of looking at things. Trying to make sense of it is just going to fuck you up."

Lou looked at his companion. "Too late, I see, for that piece of advice," he said wryly as he passed his napkin over to Josh who was trying to dab himself dry. After mopping himself up, Josh looked around for a bin.

"Here, give it to me," Lou said. He grabbed the wad of tissue from Josh, squeezed it into a tight ball, and tossed it overhand into a receptacle twenty yards away. "Three pointer!" he said with satisfaction.

Suddenly serious, he placed a meaty paw over Josh's hand, which was resting on the table. "Whichever way this situation turns out, buddy, it's going to end up breaking your heart. It burns me up to see that happen to you."

The display of concern from such an unlikely quarter caused Josh to experience a flood of emotion. He felt himself beginning to tear up. Hurriedly he got to his feet.

"Thanks for the concern, Lou. It's appreciated. We should be getting back. Webster is going to be looking for a shoulder to cry on."

Lou eyed him shrewdly. "Sure, let's make like babies and head outta here."

As they made the short walk back to the office, Josh thought about what Lou had said. Scarcely a month had passed since his arrival in Manila, but he felt his whole worldview had been turned upside down. Rita had seen to that. What was he going to say when he saw her again tomorrow? How was he going to be able to comfort her? As Lou had pointed out, getting on his high horse and ranting about the cruel injustice of it all wouldn't bring the boy back. He had to be supportive of whatever the family decided and focus on helping Rita cope with her grief.

Josh was startled to find Mark Webster pouring himself a stiff whiskey when he entered his office. It was just past 9:30 in the morning.

"I know, I know," his boss said irritably, "but it's five o'clock somewhere, and I need something to steady my nerves before I have to break the news of this latest debacle to headquarters." He bent back a sip. "I don't even want to think how the clients are going to react. IBM is flying a couple of their best guys over but they're not sure they can repair the machine. If they can't, it's going to be more than three weeks before they can get a replacement here and operational."

Holy fuck, we're screwed if that happens, Josh thought. "I'm sure it's not as bad as it looks," he said, trying to sound as positive as possible.

Webster was eyeing a box of donuts as he asked, "Any idea yet of how the downtime will impact our software delivery schedule?"

"Lou's working on that right now, Mark. Hard to say, but I've got to tell you that it's not a one-for-one slippage. It's going to impact the projects' critical path disproportionately."

"I don't know what the fuck you just said even means, Steinberg. When will you be able to come up with dates?"

"Give us 'til the end of the day to come up with something," Josh said firmly, with a lot more confidence than he felt.

"Just in time to get my ass handed to me by Corporate when they come to work," Webster said dejectedly. Suddenly his mood changed. "Why are you still standing there? Get out of here and get me some answers. Don't even thinking of going home until you do."

"Yes, boss," Josh said, and beat a hasty retreat for the door.

It was after 9 at night by the time Josh got home. He found Rita in the kitchen, sorting out the contents of the fridge.

"The milk is past its due date and the strawberries have mould all over them. Do you never check these things, Joshua?" she said irritably.

"It's been pretty busy at work," he replied defensively.

She turned toward him. He could see she was crying. He went over and pulled her to him.

"You don't need to be doing that now," he said.

"I know," she replied. "It's silly, but I have to keep myself busy or I'll go mad."

He walked her over to the couch. They sat down together. He turned toward her and held both her hands in his. "Was the funeral very difficult for you?" he asked.

"The funeral? No, not really," she sighed. "The priest was very consoling and everyone in our village was incredibly supportive. You forget for a while the way he died while all that's going on. Down there it all seemed unreal somehow. But now I'm back in the city with the streets and the traffic. I'm just so angry, Joshua."

He could feel her nails digging into his palms and tried not to wince with the pain. "You know I'm here for you, Rita. I'll do anything I can to help you through this."

She pulled her hands away and looked at him with a mixture of anguish and annoyance. "And what exactly does that mean?"

Josh was startled. "It means I love you."

"Love. Is that what this is?" She looked around the room. "I'm your paid companion for the time you're over here. I warm your bed at night. Don't tell me that you love me, not now. It just makes me feel sick to my stomach, listening to the lies."

"Listen, I know you're distraught with everything that's just happened, but we have feelings for each other. That was true before any of this happened, and it's true now. You know it." Josh felt his voice rising.

Rita looked at him wearily. "You're a nice man, and in your way, a kind man. The real truth is that this relationship is one of convenience for you. When your assignment is over you will go back to Boston and your life. I live in the Philippines. I am a Filipina. This *is* my life. The poverty, the corruption, the squalor—it's my past, my present, and my future. I have to learn to live with it, but right now that's incredibly hard. So unless you're saying you want to marry me..." She saw the look on his face and gave a sarcastic laugh. "No, I didn't imagine you were. I'm very tired, Joshua. I need to go to bed. I'll see about moving out tomorrow."

Josh felt as if he'd been gut punched. "Rita, I don't know what to say to you right now. We've only known each other a month and you're talking about marriage? I need time to get my head around everything that's happened. You talk as if I can just go back to the States and forget all about what's happened to me over here, to forget about you? Well, I'm not going to be able to do that."

He stood up and started pacing the room in his agitation. Finally, he said, "Listen, you should go to bed. I'll sleep on the sofa. I need to be up early tomorrow for work anyway. We can talk about this tomorrow." He looked at her plaintively. "Promise me you'll still be here when I come home tomorrow night?"

Without answering, she rose, went into the bedroom, and closed the door behind her.

Chapter Sixteen

"That fucker Junio has attacked a day early. He's screwed everything up!" Andres Soledad sounded hysterical. It was three in the morning. Bongo fumbled the phone receiver from his bedside locker to his ear and sat bolt upright in bed.

"What are you talking about, Andres? You need to get a grip." Bongo cursed silently under his breath.

"Jamie Junio and his commandos were assigned to blow up the communication towers at Tagaytay. He was supposed to go tomorrow but he struck too early. Worse yet, he and a number of his men have been captured."

Bongo now understood why Soledad was so rattled. "When was he taken? How much does he know?"

Soledad spoke hurriedly. "A couple of hours ago. He doesn't know the whole plan, but he knows enough to alert the government that there's a coup attempt."

"So, what do we do? Go ahead or abort?" Bongo's mind was already racing with hastily concocted plans to go into hiding or flee the country.

"I just got off the phone with Gregorio Honasan. He says we go unless we hear to the contrary. We've moved up the schedule for some of the targets to tonight, but you're still a go for tomorrow at 7 a.m. It's just not possible to scramble the logistics any faster."

"It's not too smart to be talking over the phone like this, Andres," Bongo said irritably.

"I know, Bongo, but it's our only option given what's just happened. Proceed as planned unless I contact you again. Good luck." Soledad rang off.

"What's going on? Who was that on the phone, Bongo?" His mother's anxious voice echoed from his parents' bedroom down the landing.

"Nothing, Nanay. Just some drunk dialled the wrong number. You can go back to sleep."

Bongo lit a cigarette and thought hard about his next moves. He knew Jamie Junio. The guy was thick as two planks. It did not surprise him in the slightest that the idiot had got the date wrong. The question was, what would he tell his captors and how soon?

Later that day, he was supposed to be placing bombs in garbage bins around the fort. He would be at his most vulnerable. He would monitor the news bulletins and look for signs of heightened security at the fort. If he heard or saw anything remotely suspicious, the plotters could go fuck themselves. He would head for the countryside and lie low. He got no sleep for the rest of the night.

On his way to work that morning, Bongo scanned the stations on his car radio for news of the attack on the communication towers. The reports confined themselves to detailing the time of the attack, the extent of the damage, and what disruption had been caused. There was no attribution in the public broadcasts as to who had perpetrated the assault. The line was that investigations were ongoing.

At Fort Bonifacio, he could see no evidence of heightened security. Certainly, there were no searches going on. The explosives and radio transmitter to detonate them were in a rucksack in the back of his jeep. The guard at the entrance gave his vehicle only a cursory glance before waving him through.

Bongo was distracted all morning. *What are the authorities doing?* he kept asking himself. Even supposing Junio and his captured men were holding up under interrogation, it seemed crazy to Bongo that the security forces had not increased their alert level.

The garbage trucks made their rounds at 11 a.m. as usual. At noon, palms sweaty and throat dry, he went out to his jeep, grabbed one of the lunch bags, sat on a bench, ate his sandwich, and then casually dropped the bag into the first of the bins he had earmarked. His devices would make a loud bang with a lot of smoke. They did not have lethal intent. The whole idea was to capture the fort with minimal casualties. Throughout the course of the afternoon, he repeated the performance. His fellow workers just assumed he was taking cigarette breaks. At last, he was finished.

That's the hard part done. Even if the plot was discovered now, evidence of his complicity would just be swept up and discarded with the trash. The explosives would end up buried harmlessly in some landfill. There was nothing to do now but go home and wait for the following morning.

But once home, Bongo found it impossible to settle. The adrenaline rush from planting the bombs would not subside. He thought about going for a few beers but decided against it. He needed to keep a clear head. In the end, he went to his local gym and subjected himself to a gruelling workout, which culminated in his taking out his aggression on the punching bag. He showered and ate a sandwich at a local neighbourhood stall. There was still no way he could just go home to bed. He was too wound up.

Fuck it, he thought, and went to a nearby phone booth.

He dialled the contact number Andres Soledad had given him. "It's Bongo," he said when Andres answered. "What's going on?"

"We're underway!" Soledad was exultant. "We've just seized Villamor Airbase. There was hardly any resistance. We have the commanding general of the air force trapped in his office. We've also secured the Manila domestic air terminal. We're moving to seize the other military airbases, and the north and south port terminals of Manila Bay as we speak. Where are you, Bongo? I need to be able to reach you. The timeline for the attack on Fort Bonifacio is being moved up."

"Fuck's sake, Andres. Moved up when?"

"A few hours from now. I can't give you the precise time."

"I'll join you wherever you are, Andres. That way there's no chance of us not being able to connect with each other." There was a pause at the other end of the line.

"Meet me at Villamor Airbase. We're setting up a command-and-control centre there. You can pick up a military field radio and get into position at the fort for when we launch the attack."

It was on the tip of his tongue to ask why he hadn't been issued a field radio in the first place, but all Bongo said was, "I'll be there in forty minutes."

Armed marines were guarding the entrance to the airbase when Bongo pulled up. He showed his ID, they consulted a list, and then waved him through without incident. As he approached the main building, Bongo could hear the sound of sporadic gunfire coming from the direction of the international airport terminal building, which was located some half-mile away and which shared a runway with the military airfield. After some confusion, he tracked down Andres Soledad. The lieutenant was deep in conversation with two other officers, gesticulating toward a huge map of the Manila Metro area arrayed with brightly coloured markers indicating the disposition of coup and government forces.

The room they were in was on the second floor of the main building. A bank of desks with telephones were arrayed in a horseshoe around the map, each station manned by a soldier. A runner was constantly moving around the desks and collecting the slips of paper being generated by those on the phones. These he passed on to two officers in charge of updating the map. Bongo moved himself into Soledad's line of sight and waved. Soledad, recognising him, turned quickly away from the other two officers and hurried over.

"What's the shooting about?" Bongo asked. The flashes of gunfire could be seen in the distance outside the windows.

"Some skirmishing between us and government troops at the international airport. We've established a perimeter around the runways to stop flights landing or taking off," Soledad said calmly.

There was a roar of engines outside. Soledad cocked his head. "Hear that?"

Bongo shrugged. "It's just a plane taking off."

Soledad smiled grimly. "It's a bomber on its way to the presidential palace."

Bongo was stunned. "You're going to blow up Corazon Aquino? I thought the idea was just to capture her."

"Capture or kill. It comes to the same thing. If we neutralise the civilian and military leadership of the administration, there are plenty of Marcos loyalists in the upper echelons who will be happy to switch allegiance and throw their lot in with us."

Soledad gestured toward the map. "This is where things stand. We have Villamor Airbase and the commanders of Aguinaldo and Mactan airbases have sided with us. A team of marines from here are on their way to Quezon City to seize control of the two major

TV stations. We also have control of both piers of Manila Bay. The government has been slow to respond. But that won't last. It's critical we secure Fort Bonifacio. I've just heard from Honasan. Our guys will be ready at 3 a.m. That's when you explode your devices."

"We were going to wait until the shifts changed," Bongo muttered.

"I know, but we can't give the government time to call in reinforcements. General Jose Zumel is in charge of the attack. Report to him after you've done your job. Anything else you need to know?" Soledad was already turning away.

"No, I'm clear. I could use some weaponry though," Bongo answered.

Soledad grabbed a paper and pen from one of the desks and scribbled briefly. "Show this to the guard at the door. He'll direct you where to go. Good luck." Soledad went back to the board.

Twenty minutes later, Bongo was fighting traffic on his way back to the fort. He had equipped himself with an M14 assault rifle, a grenade vest, several hundred rounds of ammunition, and a helmet. *That, along with my service revolver, should just about cover it.*

The pace of the city proceeded as usual, so far as he could tell. There was nothing on the radio to suggest a coup was underway.

Bongo pulled his jeep into a side street near the fort and looked at his watch. It was just after 11 p.m. There were four hours to wait. He set his watch alarm for 2:15 and willed himself to sleep.

He was alert at the first beep of his alarm. The transmitter to detonate the devices was hidden under a couple of blankets. He transferred it to his rucksack and then, armed only with his service revolver, made his way cautiously toward the perimeter of the fort.

As he approached, he caught sight of a company of Scout Rangers in their distinctive black uniforms poised on one of the side streets. Bongo considered identifying himself but thought better of it.

We'll see how this assault pans out. If they succeed, I take credit for the bombs going off and I'm a hero. If they fail, I just melt away into the night.

Giving the company a wide berth, he zigzagged in a crouching run until he found cover at the base of a tree that stood just outside a wall of the fort. The signal from his detonator would be attenuated by buildings, and he wanted to be sure they went off.

At 3 a.m. precisely, Bongo depressed the button on the transmitter. Almost instantaneously, a series of loud explosions rent the air. From his vantage point, Bongo could see the company of Rangers racing for the fort, the lead soldiers firing short rifle bursts as they went.

Klaxons were going off, and floodlights illuminated the fort's approaches. Two guards attempted to fire on the attackers and went down in a hail of bullets. In less than twenty minutes, it was all over and the sounds of gunfire ceased. Bongo went back to the jeep and strapped on his M14 for appearance's sake. Then he sauntered up to the guard post and identified himself.

"Lieutenant Bongo Cruz, reporting for duty," he said jauntily, ignoring the hostile and suspicious looks the soldiers guarding the gate gave him. "I'm the guy who set off the firecrackers for you. I have orders to report to General Zumel."

"It's okay, that's Bongo Cruz. I recognise him. He's one of us." The intervention came from an officer who came out of the guard post to see what was going on.

"General Zumel has taken over the superintendent's office. You know where it is?"

Bongo nodded and turned in the direction of the administration building. As he walked across the quadrangle, there was a flurry of shots far to his left—soldiers shooting in the air. Then a rustle of movement not thirty yards away. Two of the fort's defenders who had been hiding in a stairwell decided to make a break for it. They crossed in front of him, crouched and ran. None of the raiding party were making any move to stop them, waiting, it seemed, for orders to shoot.

Useless fuckers, Bongo thought disgustedly. In one fluid movement, he dropped to one knee, took aim, and brought the two men down in a hail of bullets. As he walked past them, he looked at their faces and recognised one of them. The boyish face had a look of astonishment in death. He had shared a cigarette with the kid on several occasions while on coffee break. Their last conversation, he'd congratulated the boy after he confided that his girlfriend had just agreed to marry him. *I guess now she'll have to find someone else to marry.*

"I'll leave you to clean up the mess," he said to one of the guards who had come running over and was staring down at the two dead men in disbelief. "I have to report to the General."

If Bongo expected to be congratulated by Zumel on his successful diversionary tactic, he was soon disabused of the notion. The general was in a foul mood. He acknowledged Bongo's reporting for duty with a grunt and then burst out in exasperation.

"This is turning into a shit show. First, we miss capturing Cacanando. He got away minutes before we could completely secure the perimeter. Now I've just been told we didn't manage to take out the bitch in the bombing run on the palace. She's been on television, for God's sake. So much for decapitating the leadership."

Bongo understood the reference to Manuel Cacanando. He was the commanding general of the army and headquartered at the fort. *The bitch* was shorthand for Corazon Aquino.

Bongo saw no point in getting caught up in the recriminatory rant. "What do we do now, General? What are my orders, sir?"

"We prepare to defend the fort. The Aquino people are not just going to let us sit here. You know this complex. Take some men and scour the place. Make sure there are no loyalist holdouts hiding anywhere."

Bongo saluted smartly and got out of Zumel's way.

As he walked out into the yard and prepared to dragoon a security detail, Bongo digested what Zumel had told him. He factored this latest intelligence with the much more positive assessment he had received from Soledad. So far, the coup was finely balanced between success and failure. The outcome would be decided in the next 48 hours. He frowned as he considered his options should it turn out he had backed the losing side.

Chapter Seventeen

Josh woke up and looked at his watch. It was past 11 a.m. *Shit, I'm going to be late.* He had been at the office until close to midnight the evening before.

His boss wanted to meet him and Lou for lunch at the Peninsula Hotel to discuss furloughing some of the staff while the mainframe was under repair. He wanted the discussion held offsite due to its sensitivity.

Josh pulled the curtains and looked out at the street. Traffic appeared to be flowing normally. There had been reports on the radio that some sort of military disturbance was taking place, but when Josh had asked Lou about it, he was dismissive.

"Just some sort of local squabble. It never affects the expat community. The Filipinos know which side their bread is buttered on. No need to get your knickers in a twist over it, buddy."

Josh wasn't entirely convinced, but Lou had lived in the country a lot longer than he, and the work crisis was already enough to occupy his energies. He dressed hurriedly, went outside, and hailed a cab. En route to the Peninsula, he quizzed the driver about the security situation.

"There is a coup attempt against President Aquino's government, sir," the cabbie said matter-of-factly.

"What?" Josh was startled.

"It is to be expected, sir. She has lost a lot of her popularity. When there was an attempt to depose her three years ago, people poured onto the streets here in Manila to defend her. This time we're staying home to see who comes out on top."

"But is it going to be safe to remain in the city?" Josh asked anxiously.

"Nothing to worry about, sir. It's really going to be up to the military as to who they support this time."

Certainly, as they drove through the city, Josh could see no evidence of unrest. Life was going on as normal.

The lunch dragged on for over three hours with nothing much resolved. They war-gamed various scenarios, but since they were all contingent on how long it would take to bring the mainframe back, they could make no firm decisions. In the end, they settled on furloughing some of the more junior staff. It would have a minimal impact on the budget overruns, but it would free up some managerial time.

Mark Webster was alternately despondent about the project and concerned about the coup. "Headquarters is not going to like the notion of political instability. We're on thin ice as it is. And now we have this coup nonsense. I can't make up my mind whether to put

Edie and the kids back on a plane to the States. I'm not real thrilled about sticking around myself if it comes to it."

Josh and Lou walked him out to his car at the end of the interminable meal and watched as its driver steered gingerly into traffic.

"There he goes. Our gutless wonder of a leader," Lou said with contempt. "I don't know about you, but I could do with a drink, or several."

Josh grunted his agreement, and they made a beeline for the bar in the foyer.

At Fort Bonifacio, General Zumel was incandescent.

"The traitorous whore has called in the Americans to prop her up. Their F-4 jets have taken control of the airspace and grounded our planes. I'm being told she even encouraged them to bomb us but they refused to do it. All the fence sitters in the military have rowed in behind her now that the Yanks have got in on the act. The coup has failed."

Bongo Cruz was one of the officers gathered around the general at the impromptu briefing. The mood in the room was grim.

"Are we going to surrender, General?" It was his aide-de-camp. No one else would have had the courage to ask such a question of the mercurial Zumel.

"Not yet," Zumel answered. "If we stay here we'll be overwhelmed, and this site gives us no leverage. We need to relocate to a more valuable asset. It will give us something to bargain with when the time comes."

Zumel squared his shoulders and drew himself up to his full height, a diminutive five-foot-two. "The orders are to move into Makati and take up defensive positions there. It's the business district, so Aquino and her cronies will have no interest in seeing it turned into a war zone. We need to secure vantage points in several of the high-rises that overlook the main thoroughfares. Rizal and Ayala avenues for sure." Zumel focused his gaze on one of the assembled officers. "Captain Gomez, you and your men take the intersection of Ayala and Buendia."

In quick succession, he went through his captains, reeling off street names and intersections. It was an impressive tour de force. Zumel wanted to convey confidence and a sense of control of the situation, and he was having the desired effect. Bongo found himself assigned to the cohort responsible for securing the intersection of Ayala and Makati avenues.

As the platoons formed up in the square, ready to move out, Bongo reflected on what he had heard in the briefing. The bad news was that he was on the losing side. It had been a close thing, but the intervention of the Americans had been decisive. On the other hand, while Aquino had succeeded militarily, her decision to ask for outside help to defeat her fellow countrymen would certainly prove disastrous for her politically. With this move, she was perpetuating the stereotype that Filipinos could not handle their own affairs, that they would always be playthings of some foreign power.

Whatever people thought of the merits of the attempted coup, they would resent her for involving the Americans. Her administration was doomed. Something might be salvaged from this situation after all if he could just keep a low profile. It was unfortunate that he had shot those two soldiers. He might be brought up on charges. *I can always claim self-defence,* he thought. *It's the fog of war, after all.*

The command to move out was given and the three companies of Scout Rangers marched out in good order toward the business district.

In the bar of the Peninsula Hotel, Josh and Lou, half drunk, were discussing their plans for Christmas and the New Year.

"I'm planning to take a trip to Phuket. There's nothing for me Stateside," Lou said. He belched. "That's enough beer for one day." He emptied his glass in one gulp and stretched backwards on his stool. "Time to get myself a real drink." He signalled to the bartender. "Glenlivet on the rocks, no ice. Make it a double." He looked at Josh inquiringly.

"I'll stick with my beer, thanks," Josh said. "I have no head for hard liquor." He scratched his chin, feeling the stubble of half a day's growth. "I was thinking of going back to Boston for the New Year. It will be cold as hell, but I'm getting a bit homesick, to be honest."

Lou looked at him shrewdly. "When a guy starts pining for home over here it generally means girlfriend trouble. You and Rita have a falling out?"

"Her brother's death has thrown her for a loop," Josh said. "She's re-evaluating her lifestyle choices, I guess. She's planning to move out."

"I did warn you," Lou said. He wrapped a sympathetic arm around Josh's shoulder. "Listen, a man's got to eat, heartbroken or not. Let's go to the steak restaurant here and have a bang-up meal. Courtesy of the company. After that, we can think about hitting the nightlife."

"I could go for a decent steak," Josh admitted. "But we'll have to see about the nightlife."

"Wuss," Lou admonished him cheerfully, and called for the tab.

An hour later, they had started to peruse the dessert menu when the first shots rang out.

"Is that a car backfiring?" Josh asked vacantly, by now thoroughly inebriated.

Lou had stiffened at the sound. "No man, it's rifle fire."

He had no sooner spoken than one of the glass windows that looked onto Makati Avenue shattered, spraying glass perilously close to a number of the diners. There followed a whine, and after that an explosion.

"And that, my son, is the sound of a mortar. What the fuck is going on?"

What moments before had been a quiet scene of people dining was now transformed into a maelstrom of frenzied panic. Men were cursing, women screaming. There was a mad rush for the door. Over a loudspeaker, the voice of a hotel manager could be heard giving instructions.

Lou climbed onto the table and bellowed, "Shut up and listen, people. They're trying to tell us what to do."

The crowd still jostled but quieted somewhat to hear the voice on the sound system. "Ladies and gentlemen, there is a military confrontation going on in the streets around us. Rebel forces have taken up positions in a number of nearby buildings. Forces loyal to the government of President Corazon Aquino are engaging them. The hotel is secure. I repeat, the hotel is secure. All exits are under guard. It is not safe to leave the building. Residents are asked to go to their rooms and stay away from the windows. If possible, use the stairs. Non-residents should make their way to the main ballroom. We will be making further announcements as the situation unfolds. Do not attempt to leave the hotel. I repeat, do not attempt to leave the hotel."

The maître d' and several waiters tried to marshal the guests into some sort of order as they exited the dining room. The sounds of panic had abated somewhat, but there were still agitated exchanges going on among the guests. Lou clambered down off the table and downed the last of his wine before pointing his finger toward the door.

"Right, our next stop is reception."

"Why?" Josh asked, confused.

"To book us a couple of rooms, for God's sake. If we're going to be stuck here, we might as well do it in comfort. I'm not going to be corralled into some lousy ballroom with a bunch of howling babies and soiled diapers. So long as this place can provide beer and pizzas we can settle in for a nice jolly coup."

"I'm worried about Rita," Josh said anxiously.

"Where is she now?" Lou asked.

"She's staying with her uncle and aunt as far as I know."

"In that case I wouldn't worry too much. She's not in Makati, and that extortionist cousin of hers sounds like a sharp operator. He'll make sure his family is kept well out of the firing line."

"I'll try and get hold of her after we've checked in," Josh said.

Up on the fifteenth floor, Philip Wentworth was in his bathrobe, dozing on his bed. The girl had just left. He had an arrangement with one of the doormen who supplied masseuses to guests that were in the know. Their massage skills left a lot to be desired, but they made up for it in other ways.

Angel was no longer answering his calls. *Fuck her,* he thought. He didn't like using the hotel whores because he worried about STDs, but this whole traffic accident thing had made him nervous, and he needed the sexual release. The explosions outside woke him. Wentworth walked over to the window and looked down.

An armoured car was trying to make its way up Makati Avenue under a hail of bullets, sparks flying from its sides. As he watched, it was hit by a missile, veered off the side of the road, and burst into flames. One of the occupants, his clothing on fire, tumbled out. The screams were audible even from hundreds of feet up.

In the background, machine gun fire chattered away. Furtive armed figures scurried from doorway to doorway along the street. Wentworth pulled himself back from his window and hurried into the bathroom where he sat on the toilet seat, shivering and sweating. That was where he was when he heard the announcement over the speaker system.

For fuck's sake. What am I going to do now? I shouldn't even be here. If it weren't for that stupid kid in the middle of the road, I'd be back home in England.

He felt sick. He got up, twisted to open the toilet seat and vomited into the bowl. Afterward, he lay slumped beside it for several minutes, his mind blank. He finally stumbled over to the bedside phone and tried calling the British Embassy. All he got was a busy signal. Wentworth was terrified and felt trapped. He turned on the TV, where Corazon Aquino was giving an address. Something about the rebels needing to surrender or die. *Incompetent sow,* he thought. *This would never have happened under Marcos.*

Chapter Eighteen

Bongo and his cohort, under the command of Captain Alejandro Mendoza, drove to their assigned intersection in the business district, encountering no government forces along the way. Two military trucks conveyed the men. The platoon carried M14s with several M79 grenade launchers and was accompanied by a mortar team with a 60mm tube. A civilian truck waited for them, loaded with ammunition and provisions. Mendoza pointed to a high-rise on Ayala Avenue a few hundred yards from the intersection with Makati.

"We're going to secure that building, Cruz." He gestured at Bongo. "Take a squad and the mortar and clear out the occupants of the top floor. Use force if you have to, but don't shoot anyone if you can help it. We don't want to alienate the locals. I'll take the rest of the platoon and secure the entrances and exits at street level." He pointed at the truck. "General Zumel has been pre-positioning supplies in Makati for the past couple of days. He's a wily bastard. Once we have this place under control, we need to unload what he's given us and get set to defend our intersection from positions at street level, on the roof, and the upper floor. Look lively. We're not going to have much time before the government troops are on top of us."

Bongo picked a sergeant, told him to alert his squad, and as a group they rushed the main entrance to the building.

The security guards at the reception looked on helplessly as Bongo and his men swept in, closely followed by Mendoza and the rest of the platoon. Bongo pointed his M14 menacingly at the guards. "I'd get out of here, fellas, if you don't want to end up with a bullet in your head." The men fled out onto the street.

Three elevators serviced the building, two reserved for residents, the third for freight. Bongo posted two men in front of them. "Anyone coming down leaves the building immediately. No one goes up. The rest of you are coming with me in the service elevator. We need to clear out the top floor."

He surveyed the hallway when they got to the top. An exit door marked a stairwell that led to the roof, and he told his mortar crew to go up and sight their weapons. There were four apartments to check on this floor.

"Right," he said. "We'll tackle those two first. They face into Ayala."

"What do we do if there's no answer when we knock?" one of his men asked anxiously.

"For Chrissake." Bongo hammered on one of the doors with the butt of his machine gun. "You in there. This is the military. We are requisitioning your apartment. You have one minute to open up or we'll break the door down. Open up, goddamn it. Like that!" he barked at the soldier who had questioned him.

There was the sound of a chain being pulled back behind the door in front of him. It swung open to reveal a frightened elderly Filipina. He pushed past her and surveyed the living room, gun at the ready.

"Two men, you and you, check the other rooms."

"Please, sir," the old woman spoke in a trembling voice. "There is only me and my husband. He is resting in the bedroom. He is very unwell. He has prostate cancer. Please do not upset him."

Bongo was unimpressed. "Do these windows on the street side open, woman? Your husband had best shift himself in a hurry or I'll give him a kick up the backside that will do nothing good for his fucking prostate."

The woman collapsed, sobbing at his feet. He stepped over her and followed his men into the bedroom where a shrunken elderly man lay cowering under the bedclothes.

"Get this walking corpse and his caterwauling wife out of here while I go see how the evictions are going in the other apartments," he ordered his men.

Next door, he found three of his men lounging around the doorway smoking.

"What's going on here?" he demanded.

"It's a mother with two young kids. Her husband is at work," said one of the men. "She asked if she could pack a few things before she left."

Bongo punched the wall with his fist, just missing the man's head. "Are you fucking kidding me? I told you to clear the apartment now, not whenever some bitch has finished selecting her wardrobe. Get her and the brats out immediately, do you hear me? The government could be on us any minute. We need to take up positions."

Bongo looked venomous. The men raced to do his bidding. Within twenty minutes, Bongo had a mortar and rifles trained on the intersection from the roof and the two forward-facing apartments. He radioed down to Captain Mendoza, who was pleased with the progress.

"Good job, Cruz. Have a couple of your guys come down and start ferrying some of these supplies back up. Have the men eat something while we have the chance. I don't think we'll have a very long wait before Aquino's troops pay us a visit."

Mendoza was right. Less than an hour later, a column of armoured cars made its way up Ayala Avenue. It was clearly some form of coordinated incursion. The sound of explosions and gunfire could be heard close by. Pedestrians scrambled for safety, either dodging up side streets or seeking shelter in nearby buildings. As the lead vehicle passed the front door, it was struck by a grenade launched by one of Mendoza's men at street level.

Bongo gave the order, and from their positions, his men laid down a withering hail of fire from above. A mortar shell hit the second car in the column, causing it to burst into flames. The lead car veered off the street, lodging in a hedge and the column stopped. Elements started to disperse into the surrounding neighbourhood. From his vantage point on the roof, Bongo surveyed the situation, his face grim.

"So far so good," he said with satisfaction. The feeling was short-lived. A black dot appeared above the horizon in front of him, and he heard the distant sound of propeller blades. He stared at the object until it became recognisable. "It's a helicopter gunship. Everyone off the roof, now!" he yelled.

The last man barely made it through the safety door before the roof was wracked by a hail of machine gun fire. Squinting through a crack, Bongo saw an M79-launched grenade narrowly miss the hovering aircraft. The pilot, sensing his vulnerability, veered away as Bongo and his men retreated to the upper floor apartments.

In one, the window was completely blown out, glass scattered everywhere. A soldier, covered in blood, screamed in agony, a huge gash in his right leg.

"And that," Bongo said to no one in particular, "is why we don't need civilians in the line of fire." He took a closer look at the injured man. "If we don't tourniquet his leg this poor bastard is going to bleed to death. Someone get a sheet off the bed. Tear it into strips." As he spoke, he grabbed a lace doily off a sideboard, made a pad of it and clapped it to the wound. He grabbed the arm of the man nearest him and pulled him down.

"Keep pressure on this. I need to find something in the kitchen." Bongo bounded over to the kitchen and started opening drawers, tipping their contents indiscriminately onto the floor. Eventually he found what he was looking for: the sharpening steel of a carving set.

He hurried back to the wounded man. An outstretched hand offered him a strip from the torn-up sheet which Bongo wrapped around the man's thigh, and with the sharpening steel, applied torsion to staunch the flow of blood. He stood up to survey his handiwork.

"He'll do for now. He'll have to. Sweep up all this broken glass before our feet are cut to shreds. I need to report to Mendoza."

No further attempts were made on their position the rest of that day. Arrangements were made to transfer Bongo's wounded man and a couple of the other soldiers injured at street level to a local hospital.

That evening, though weary, Bongo made a call to his father.

"Where are you, Bongo?" The tone in his father's voice smacked more of irritation than concern. "We've had the military police here looking for you."

Bongo was surprised. "What did they want?" There was no way the government could be tracking down every insurgent so quickly.

"They say you shot two men in cold blood at Fort Bonifacio. You were recognised and reported."

Bongo was defiant. "They were armed. They posed a threat to me and my men. I dealt with it. If they were slow off the mark, that's not my fault."

"Be that as it may, you're a wanted man, Bongo. Don't come near the house. Are you injured?" His father asked almost as an afterthought.

"Not so far, Tatay. Thanks for asking though." Bongo's tone was sarcastic. His father chose to ignore it.

"The coup has clearly failed. You're going to have to go to ground for a while. I don't think it's going to be enough to hide out in the provinces, Bongo. We are a known family of Marcos supporters. The government will be looking to make an example of you. They will actively hunt you if you remain in the country. We may need to send you abroad for a while until all this dies down."

"And where would you suggest I go?" Bongo was dubious.

"Indonesia or Vietnam. I'm going to have to ask around, call in a couple of favours." His father's voice was pensive.

"Well, just right now I'm kind of preoccupied with not getting my head shot off by government troops. You don't need to know where I am exactly; in fact, it's better you don't in case they interrogate you again." Bongo felt a surge of irritation. "I'm not thrilled about going into exile, just so you know."

"You backed a losing horse, son. I can't say I blame you, but there will be consequences."

"How is Rita holding up?"

His father's response was exasperated. "Mooning about the place dressed in black, going to Mass and saying a lot of rosaries. Your mother has got in on the act. The place is like a funeral home. It's driving me crazy if you must know. Anyway, none of this lamenting is going to bring the boy back. How far have you got with the guy who ran him over?"

"I haven't talked to him in the last 24 hours for obvious reasons. I'll chase him down after I hang up and make sure he doesn't think this coup mess has changed anything."

"You do that, Bongo." His father's voice finally warmed. "Phone in a couple of days. It's going to take me at least that long to get something organised for you."

His father rang off.

Rita let herself into her aunt's house and slipped quietly upstairs to the bedroom where she was staying. She had no wish to encounter either her uncle or aunt. She sensed she was wearing out her welcome with her uncle. He wanted his household back to normal. She could understand where he was coming from. Eddie was not his blood relation, and he had agreed to take the boy in only to please his wife. Her aunt Maria had been genuinely fond of Eddie. She broke into paroxysms of weeping every time his name was mentioned or she happened to glance at his photograph in the dining room, which she had flanked with two lighted candles since his death.

Wearily, Rita folded her black mantilla and put it in her bedside drawer, together with her white gloves and rosary beads. She lay on the bed, fully clothed and stared vacantly at the ceiling before closing her eyes and letting her weight sink into the mattress. Emotionally she felt numb. Physically, every motion, however slight, seemed to be a huge effort. Her mind was agitated, her thoughts erratic. Fleeting images of Eddie laid out in his coffin, or her parents distraught at the graveside, jostled with those of the apartment where she had been staying, and the bar where she worked. *What sort of life am I leading? How have I arrived at such a place?*

Then there was the American. She had genuine feelings for him. He could be funny and had a wide-eyed innocence and enthusiasm about him that she found both refreshing and endearing. For all his protestations of love, however, she was almost certain that for him, it was just a dalliance. Though there was some small part of her that hoped against hope there was something more between them.

How pathetic I am. Just another foolish Filipina imagining that some rich foreigner would rescue her from a life of poverty and exploitation.

As a schoolgirl she had always considered herself different in some way from her friends and neighbours. In truth, Rita acknowledged sadly, she was just a tired stereotype, indistinguishable from tens of thousands of other young girls caught up in the sex trade. Joshua was generous and kind. She was deeply touched by his offer to accompany her to Eddie's funeral in her village, even if it was totally impractical. Maybe he was indeed different. She had been mean and cruel to him at their last meeting. Any young man would have been shocked and taken aback at being catapulted into a family tragedy like hers after so short an acquaintance. She had put pressure on him to make a serious commitment to her. He hadn't said no, he'd just asked for more time. It could have been a genuine reaction on his part.

It was not Joshua's fault that her life was a mess. She had managed to bring that about all by herself. He was the product of a prosperous society with no comprehension of what constant hand-to-mouth existence did to the human spirit. Her sense of urgency to have some stability and financial security was not something he could relate to. She really needed to give him a chance. He was her slender hope of a way out. She needed to see him again.

Rita got up, made her way downstairs, and put on a light raincoat. Ever so quietly, she tried to open the front door, but her aunt's voice stopped her in her tracks.

"Rita, where are you going? You've only just got back."

"I was just going to have a cup of coffee with girlfriends, Aunt," Rita lied.

"We're in the middle of a coup, you foolish girl. The streets aren't safe. Going to church to say prayers for poor Eddie is one thing, it's just around the corner, but waltzing off for coffee with your friends? I can't take the worry of it. On top of everything else this will kill me. Raoul," she wailed, "tell her she can't go."

Her uncle, who had been in the bathroom, came down the stairs, buckling his belt as he descended. "You're going nowhere, Rita, do you hear me? If you do go out that door, you'll find it locked when you come back. I won't have you upsetting your aunt like this, you stupid girl."

For a moment Rita thought of defying him and leaving, but where would she go? She could endure the humiliation of going back to Joshua and asking to stay with him again after just announcing she was moving out. She could go back to the cramped room above the bar with the other girls. Neither option was appealing. She was trapped.

"I don't want to upset you, Aunt. I can wait until the streets are safer."

"You can make yourself useful, girl," said her uncle. "Fix us something for dinner. Your aunt could do with a break." He reached for the newspaper and settled himself in his armchair.

"Will Bongo be joining us for dinner?" Rita asked.

"Your cousin is fulfilling his military duties. He will not be home," her uncle snapped irritably, glancing at his wife to gauge her reaction.

"Blessed Mother, keep him safe," was all she said as she crossed herself, stifling a sob.

Rita was not convinced by the explanation. Bongo had gone to ground. She had been in the house when the military police stopped by the previous day. Her uncle had passed the visit off to his wife as being a routine check to see that he and his family were safe, given his status as a citizen of note. Rita knew that was a lie. Everyone knew that the Cruz family were Marcos loyalists. It was likely that either Bongo or his father was suspected of being part of the coup. Rita's money was on her cousin. Her uncle was too cautious a man to take the risk of getting actively involved.

Rita retreated to the kitchen and set about making the evening meal. She found some chicken thighs in the fridge and decided to make a chicken adobo with rice.

As she prepared the marinade, she considered how best to get hold of Joshua in the middle of this untimely coup attempt. Even though it was directed at Corazon Aquino, a woman, Rita regarded the disturbance as fundamentally male-inspired and male-driven. Women were inevitably the losers when something like this happened. They stood to lose their husbands or their adult sons. The precarious livelihoods that kept bread on the table for them and their younger children invariably suffered. While the men pursued power and self-aggrandisement, it was the women who were left to pick up the pieces.

Rita poured the marinade over the chicken and set it to one side. Ideally the meat should have been left to absorb the sauce for several hours, but thirty minutes would have to do. As she washed the rice before putting it in the stove to simmer, Rita thought about how best to contact Joshua. It was going to be a loss of face for her to have to make the first move, but she did not want to run the risk of waiting for him to reach out to her. Given the way their last conversation had ended he might never do so. She decided against having it out over the phone. She needed to see him in person. So absorbed was Rita in her quandary that she let the water boil off the rice and burned it. With a heavy sigh, she threw out the batch and started over again. She put the chicken on simmer over a low heat.

I'll write a note asking him to meet me at the church, Rita thought. *That way, if he doesn't show I'll know it's over.* She considered how the note could be delivered. There was no way her aunt would agree to her absenting herself to cross the city. The mail could be slow and unreliable. She had to know that Joshua received it. As she prepared to call her aunt and uncle for the evening meal, Rita decided to reach out to one of her friends, have them meet her at Mass the following morning, and hand deliver her letter to Joshua at his apartment.

Chapter Nineteen

The morning of the second day of the rebel takeover of Makati saw the staff of the Peninsula Hotel trying to cope with the fear, frustration, and anger of the trapped residents. During the previous evening and throughout the night, there had been sounds of sporadic gunfire and occasional explosions. This had served to fray the nerves of everyone in the building. It was proving particularly harrowing for those with infants and young children.

A young mother was berating the man stationed at the concierge desk. "The hotel shop has run out of diapers. How am I supposed to keep my six-month-old clean and dry?"

"I'm very sorry, madam, but it's not safe right now for our suppliers to drive the streets. The hot water still works, and you do have a sink and a bath in your room."

The woman looked at him with abhorrence. "That's positively disgusting. Why are the streets unsafe? What is your government doing about the situation? It's a disgrace. This is the last time I set foot in the Philippines; I can tell you that."

The hotel switchboard was overwhelmed by guests looking for an outside line. The foreigners were desperate to get through to their embassies, and everyone else was trying to reach friends and family. Lou and Josh arranged to meet up in the lobby. In contrast to those around him, Lou seemed in excellent spirits.

"I don't know about you, sport, but they gave me a suite last night, complete with a well-stocked mini bar." He grinned. "The only drawback was they couldn't supply me with a masseuse. Oh, and another complaint, I wasn't able to have a swim this morning. They've closed the pool as a security precaution. They really are pulling out all the stops, safety-wise," he added sarcastically. "Let's go see what they have for breakfast."

Josh was nonplussed. He had spent the night in a state of considerable anxiety. The whole situation had a nightmarish quality about it. He had been catapulted from a safe and peaceful life in Boston to a war zone in the space of a few short weeks.

"I don't know how you can be so calm about this. People are getting killed out there."

Josh was in no mood to eat, but he felt cast adrift and needed his friend's company to have a sense of security. He reluctantly trailed along after Lou as he strode in the direction of the breakfast buffet.

"Out there is the operative word, my friend," Lou responded over his shoulder without looking back. "We stay away from the windows, we're safe enough." He surveyed the display of fruit on offer. "No fresh pineapple. I mean to say, it's just not acceptable in a top-class establishment, coup or no coup. Standards must be maintained. Oh, well. I'll just have to make do with fresh mango."

"I think you're being awfully flippant," Josh said peevishly as they sat down.

Lou looked at him and shook his head. "Listen, Josh. We're helpless pawns in this situation. If we put our nose outside the door we stand a good chance of being shot or blown up. If the rebels had wanted to turn this into a hostage situation, they would have done it by now. We just keep our heads down, and at some point the authorities will figure a way of getting us out of here. All we can do is try to make the best of things. I'm going up for some bacon and eggs. You want anything?"

Josh shook his head. "I'll just stick with coffee, thanks."

Lou shrugged. "Suit yourself."

As his companion headed back to the food counter, Josh considered what he had said. It was all very well for him to posit a rational outcome to this nightmare, but the whole situation was illogical to start with. Anything might still happen. The rebels might attempt to occupy the hotel, while the government could opt to use brute force to subjugate them and start shelling indiscriminately. He and everyone else in the hotel was at risk of injury or death, no matter how much Lou fucking Holt tried to sugarcoat it. His family and friends back home would be worried sick.

Josh thought about Rita. He was concerned for her safety, but only up to a point. She was staying with family, and by all accounts they were politically well connected. It was the loss of her brother and how that was affecting her that really occupied his thoughts.

I like this girl a lot, he admitted to himself, *even if she has tried to blow me off.*

Lou returned, his plate laden with food. Josh bit his lip and refrained from making a comment. He asked the waiter to refill his coffee as he watched his friend devour everything before him.

"When we're done here what say we grab a beer, go up a couple of floors, and take a peek out on the street and see if anything is stirring," Lou said while slathering butter on a croissant.

Josh looked at him in amazement. "In the first place it's only 9 o'clock in the morning, Lou, a bit early for beer don't you think? And in the second, we're supposed to stay away from the windows."

"Don't be such a killjoy. What else have we got to do?"

"A quick look then," Josh agreed grudgingly. "Though I'll be drinking orange juice."

A window on the mezzanine level gave them a good view of Ayala Avenue. Lou had his nose pressed up against it. Josh was more circumspect and stood a few feet back. What they saw was a line of armoured vehicles. Tanks were in the lead, followed by infantry-carrying APCs farther up past the corner.

Lou whistled. "That's some serious hardware. Aquino's people look like they're done fucking around."

There was initially no movement on the street, but then the two men were treated to the incongruous sight of a group of nuns walking in procession toward the tanks. Suddenly, there was the sound of rifle fire. The nuns scattered, running.

"It's a nun shoot!" Lou said excitedly.

"For God's sake, Lou," Josh said in exasperation, "Can you take nothing seriously?"

Lou was undeterred. "How many do you think they'll bag? Three, four? What odds do you want?"

Josh turned away in disgust. "I've seen enough." He left Lou transfixed by the drama unfolding below them and headed back to his room, thinking *I was right as soon as I got here. The whole country is a fucking armpit. What the hell am I doing here?*

In another wing of the hotel, Philip Wentworth was still in bed. A half empty bottle of Scotch stood on the stand beside him. The remnants of last night's dinner lay strewn on a table. Wentworth had not bothered to leave his tray outside the suite for collection. In fact, since the building had been locked down, he had remained in his bedroom, which had no windows, and avoided his living area, which did.

Quite simply, he was terrified. The sound of gunfire and intermittent explosions acted like a cattle prod causing him to flinch involuntarily at every instance and denying him any sleep. All he could think of was how he was going to manage to escape. Multiple calls to the British Embassy had gone unanswered. He kept getting a recorded message saying the Embassy was monitoring the situation closely and working with the authorities to assure the safety of British Nationals.

The message went on to ask the caller to identify if they were a British citizen, and if so, to leave their contact information. The last part of the message discouraged callers from trying to go to the Embassy itself. Although he was already registered with them, Wentworth wanted the comfort of confirming his details. His frustration became incandescent when each time he tried to leave a message, he was told the voicemail was full. He tried getting direct hold of his contact in the Embassy, to no avail.

He's probably been on the BA flight back home with most of the rest of them at the first whiff of trouble, Wentworth thought irritably. *Save yourselves and fuck the rest of us.*

Awash in self-pity, he had not to that point phoned home, afraid that his wife might have discovered the money missing from their account. Now, goaded by loneliness and the need to talk to someone about his predicament, Wentworth placed the call and waited nervously for someone to answer.

"Greygables, Penelope Wentworth speaking."

"Hello Pen, it's Philip," Wentworth said nervously.

"Oh, it's you, Philip. Where are you speaking from?"

"I'm in Manila, Pen," he said plaintively.

"Still? I thought you would have left by now." His wife sounded almost bored.

"There's a coup going on in case you hadn't heard, my dear. It makes travel just a tad awkward."

His wife was unfazed by the sarcasm. "Now that you mention it, I did hear something about it on the news. It's unlike you to get caught with your foot in the door like that, Philip. You've always put such a premium on self-preservation."

"I'm in the middle of a war zone, Penelope. People are getting killed around me."

"Where are you exactly?" His wife sounded marginally more interested.

"I'm trapped in my suite at the Peninsula Hotel in the middle of all the fighting."

"The Peninsula. Well, that's a perfectly reputable chain. I'm sure they're taking all precautions to keep their guests safe, Philip. Apart from the undoubted inconvenience of it all, I really don't see what you're getting yourself all worked up about." She sniffed irritably. "I take it from this that you won't be making the boys' Christmas concert at the school again this year?"

"That's right, I've personally arranged a coup in the Philippines in order to get out of going to the blasted concert." There was silence at the other end of the phone. He sighed. "Please, let's stop sniping at each other, Penelope. I could do with just a little cheering up. How are the boys? What's the weather like over there? How are you, if it comes to it?"

There was a pause before his wife eventually replied. "The boys are fine, Philip, looking forward to the end of term and the Christmas holidays. We've had some light frost overnight and a dusting of snow. It's made the village look quite seasonal, a picture postcard really."

"And you, Pen, how are you?" He surprised himself by asking her again.

"I keep myself busy, Philip, as you well know. I'm going up to London next week to see *The Nutcracker* at the Royal Opera House. The vicar is organising a jumble sale in the church hall to support the Salvation Army. I'm on the committee. In fact, there's a meeting tomorrow. I'll mention your current difficulties to him, and I'm sure he'll say a prayer. You might even get a mention at Sunday's service."

Wentworth was visualising the winter scene his wife had described as she continued on. The receiver trembled in his hand, and he was engulfed by an overwhelming desire to be back home in England. He thought of his two sons, whom he had sired, provided for, but otherwise largely ignored. Remorse and regret were added to his unfamiliar maelstrom of emotion.

"There's someone at the door, Penelope." His voice choked as he came up with the excuse to cut the conversation short. "It might be news about the lockdown. I'm sorry, I have to ring off. I'll call tomorrow if I can."

He sat slumped in his chair, head in his hands. After a while he looked up and surveyed the state of disarray around him.

This won't do, old son, Wentworth said to himself. He set about piling all the dirty dishes left from room service onto the table in front of him, grabbed a laundry bag from his wardrobe, and stuffed his soiled shirts, socks, and underwear into it. He went into the bathroom, showered and shaved, and put on slacks, a T-shirt, and loafers. Finally, he phoned housekeeping and asked for his room to be made up.

If I stay locked up in here, I'll go crazy, he thought. *I need some human company.*

For all his conviction, Wentworth still hesitated before stepping into the hallway, looking around nervously before venturing toward the elevators.

Rita's companion lifted the veil of her mantilla to whisper to her as they knelt side by side in a pew in Rita's local church. "He's not there."

"What do you mean?" Rita anxiously fiddled with her rosary beads.

"His neighbour said she met Josh yesterday morning and he said he was heading downtown for a meeting at the Peninsula. He joked about it making a nice change from the office, according to her."

Rita gasped. "Holy Mother of God, Rosalie, don't you understand what that means? He's got himself caught up in the siege of Makati. He could be killed."

An older woman two rows in front of them looked around disapprovingly, gesturing them to keep silent while the priest was saying Mass. Rosalie made a hurried show of turning the pages of her prayer book, leaving Rita to rock backward and forward in agitation.

They had left on such bad terms. Rita began replaying her harsh words to Josh before she stormed off. She had a vivid memory of her last sight of him, with his expression of shock and hurt. It was like a knife in her heart. The walls of the church seemed to close in around her. She felt as if she were suffocating.

"I've got to get out of here," she whispered to Rosalie and rose to leave. The old woman in front turned around again, her look of disapproval hardening to one of open hostility as she registered Rita's intention to leave Mass early. Once outside, Rita sat down heavily on a bench in the church courtyard and tried to make sense of the intensity of emotion she had just experienced.

Why should the fate of this young American matter so much to me? I've only known him a couple of weeks. I should be more concerned about what will happen to my friends and family as a result of this attempted coup.

Her rationalisation made no difference. She was terrified for Josh. Images of him shot, lying bleeding in a street somewhere, kept flooding her mind.

Am I in love with him? Is that what this means?

Rosalie joined her on the bench, clasping both Rita's hands in her own. "You look very unwell and you're trembling. We need to get you home."

"I'll be alright in a moment," Rita responded. "It was just a bit of a shock what you told me, that's all."

"Does the boy mean that much to you?" Rosalie seemed surprised.

"We parted on bad terms. I just feel a little guilty," Rita replied evasively.

"There's not a lot you can do except perhaps pray for him to be safe."

I've just lost my brother. I can't lose him too, Rita thought. *But what can I do?*

It was too dangerous to enter the business district, and even if she managed it, she had no way of knowing what kind of reception Josh would give her. She would try phoning. It would have to be from a pay phone. There was no privacy at her aunt's house. She looked plaintively at Rosalie, who was sitting alongside her, silent, unsure how to console her friend.

"Have you any change for the phone, Rosalie? I want to try the hotel."

Rosalie looked at her dubiously. She sighed and rummaged in her purse, found some peso coins, and handed them to Rita. "There's a phone booth at the far end of the street. I need to get to work, or I'd stay with you. Will you be at Mass tomorrow?" Rita nodded. "You can let me know how you got on then. I'll say a prayer for you, Pangga."

Rita squeezed her friend's hand and hurried down the street, looking desperately for the pay phone. It was in use when she reached it. She waited impatiently for the young girl, chattering gaily with what Rita supposed was her boyfriend, to finish.

It was a long wait. Eventually, by continually trying to make eye contact with the talkative teenager, Rita managed to intimidate her into hanging up. Only when she had control of the phone did she realise she did not know the number for the Peninsula.

How could I be so stupid? It took forever for the operator to answer. Her efforts were futile. When the operator connected her, the hotel just kept giving a busy signal. Distraught, Rita returned home, avoiding her aunt's endless questions by pleading a headache and retreating to her room where she lay on her bed sobbing into the pillow.

Chapter Twenty

In the high-rise opposite the Peninsula Hotel, a weary Bongo Cruz was getting status reports from the three young soldiers he had made his team leaders. They were barely into their twenties and made Bongo feel old. Their meeting was held in the corridor of the eighteenth floor, away from all windows.

"We're okay for food. We've been scavenging the kitchens of empty apartments. The biggest problem is that we're running low on ammunition." The speaker sported a shaved head and was the most self-confident of the three. His two companions seemed happy to let him be the spokesman.

"The government forces have thrown up a steel cordon around Makati," Bongo told them. "They mean to starve us out if they can. They're not interested in a bloodbath and wholesale destruction. It would upset Corazon Aquino's foreign backers. They have too much money tied up in Makati." Bongo rubbed his chin thoughtfully. "We can't expect much by way of relief supplies. We're going to have to improvise. Let's set about making Molotov cocktails." They looked at him blankly.

"Gasoline bombs." His audience seemed none the wiser. "For Chrissake, guys," Bongo said in exasperation. "You." He stabbed with his finger at the soldier who had given him the update. "Get some containers, buckets, anything you can lay your hands on. Take a couple of guys and go down into the underground garage and syphon gasoline from the cars. You do know how to syphon gas?"

The man nodded.

"You other two, have some of your men gather up as many glass bottles as they can, milk, beer, soda, whatever you can find in the apartments. Tear up some bed sheets into strips to make fuses. We rendezvous back here in two hours. Let's hope our government friends give us a break in the meantime. We're going to set up a bomb-making factory."

The men, subdued and nervous at the outset of their encounter, took courage from Bongo's energy and assured demeanour. They scattered to execute his instructions.

Bongo turned and entered one of the apartments overlooking the street. "You, take a break. I need some privacy to make a phone call." His comments were directed at a soldier who was stationed at a window, rifle at the ready. "Be back in fifteen minutes. This isn't going to take long."

Once he had the place to himself, Bongo positioned an armchair where he could have a view of Ayala Avenue and picked up the phone. There was still a dial tone. *Good,* he thought, *they haven't cut the line yet.* He dialled his parents' number. His father answered.

"Hi Tatay, it's Bongo. Have you any news for me?"

His father got to the point immediately. "There have been developments. Your boss, Zumel, made a smart move decamping to Makati. I'm assuming that's where you are. The government is in negotiations with the coup leaders. They want a peaceful surrender. Politically, calling in the Americans has been a disaster for Aquino. It's just built a groundswell of support for her opponents. Don't get me wrong. People are not happy about the coup, but they object to government forces killing their fellow countrymen with American help."

"Will I still need to leave the country?" Bongo asked anxiously.

"They're talking amnesty. So long as you guys control Makati you have leverage. How are you holding out?" Bongo filled his father in on the situation. "You need to hang tough a few more days. The longer this drags on the worse it looks for the government. Don't fold now. They're going to have to settle, and hopefully on terms favourable to you."

His father's words buoyed Bongo's mood. The man was a shrewd political operative, and he rarely misjudged situations.

"I'm pretty sure we can hold out where I am, Tatay. It really depends on the others. I'll relay your assessment to my commander. It might help stiffen his spine."

"Do that, Bongo, and stay safe." His father rang off.

As Bongo maintained guard at the window waiting for the soldier he had relieved to return, he considered how best to strengthen his defences. He would set his men to barricading the entrance to the building. Comings and goings would need to be through the fire exit. He would post a couple of snipers there. Bongo was under no illusion that if the government put its mind to it, their position could be overwhelmed in short order. Their best hope lay in causing so much collateral damage if attacked that government forces would baulk at pressing home their advantage in the face of such destruction.

The opportunity to test his hypothesis came in the early hours of the following morning when his sentries reported an armoured car driving at speed down Ayala Avenue, along with two columns of soldiers running behind in support.

"They mean to ram the entrance!" Bongo exclaimed.

The columns broke to either side, and the men scattered to the shelter of doorways and trees. From there, they directed a withering hail of bullets at the apartment building. The driver of the armoured car jerked it around suddenly and aimed directly for the entrance.

"Now," Bongo ordered. "Let them have it!"

From the roof of the building, his men rained down Molotov cocktails on their foes. The armoured car disappeared in a sheet of flame. One of the soldiers who was using the vehicle as a shield took a direct hit and was turned into a screaming human torch.

As he writhed in the middle of the street Bongo dispassionately unslung his rifle, took careful aim, and fired. The screaming stopped. The body lay burning on the ground below.

"Better to put the poor bastard out of his misery," Bongo said. The street below was a sea of fire. The armoured car, still smoking, with scattered flames on its roof, began to reverse.

"Don't return their fire. Conserve your ammunition," Bongo ordered.

As suddenly as it had started the assault was over. His men let out a ragged cheer. "What will they do now, sir?" one of them asked.

"Remains to be seen. If they really wanted to, they could line up a couple of tanks and blast us all to kingdom come. One thing for sure, they're not going to make the same mistake twice. We must wait and see what they'll try next. Are there any casualties? Anyone hurt?" Bongo called out. No one on the roof had been injured. "I'm going down to the two lower floors to see how our guys fared down there. Keep a sharp lookout. They will be back."

In the bar of the Peninsula, Philip Wentworth ordered a Glenfiddich. The bartender was apologetic.

"Sorry sir, we're all out."

Wentworth sighed in frustration. "Well, what Scotch do you have then?"

"We still have a couple of bottles of Johnny Walker," the bartender replied, endeavouring to sound cheerful.

"Black Label?" Wentworth inquired.

"Sorry sir, only Red Label."

"It figures," Wentworth said with disgust. "Give me a large measure with a splash of soda, no ice."

Wentworth had spent the day wandering aimlessly around the hotel. Initially he had tried starting conversations with some of the other guests, but soon tired of it. No one seemed to know anything more about the situation than he could glean from the news channels, particularly CNN, which at least was in English. Most of the conversation revolved around fears for their safety, and in the case of the locals, that of their family.

Wentworth had enough worries of his own. He had neither the time nor the patience to empathise with others. The only pleasurable interlude he'd had was a half hour chatting with another Brit who seemed far more concerned about the outcome of the upcoming soccer match between arch-rivals Manchester City and Liverpool.

"We've had this guy Ferguson as manager for the past three years, and nothing to show for it. We were humiliated in September losing 5-1 to Man City, the least he can manage is a result against Liverpool."

Wentworth was not much of a soccer fan, but he played along. Talking about sport with a fellow countryman reminded him of England and home. It was late, after one in the morning, but he did not want to go back to his lonely room.

"Their liquor cabinet is running kinda low, huh?" A middle-aged man to Wentworth's left interrupted his reverie. "Bourbon is my poison of choice, but all they can offer me is Wild Turkey. They're all out of Jack Daniels. Meadows is the name, by the way. Clyde Meadows."

Wentworth introduced himself and the two struck up a conversation. After some desultory exchanges about sports— Meadows wanted to talk about American football, in which Wentworth had no interest—the conversation turned to their shared predicament, and how they were coping.

"The gunfire and shit don't bother me much," Meadows asserted. "I did a couple of tours of duty in Vietnam, so these guys running around with popguns is pretty junior league as far as I'm concerned. That's not to say it couldn't get ugly, it could. I never thought to find myself in harm's way in the middle of a shooting war again. What I regret most is not taking time to connect with my two sons. Wife and I got divorced soon after I left the service. Can't say as I blame her. I was pretty fucked up for a couple of years. She got the kids, and I didn't have much to do with them when they were growing up. To be honest, I wasn't much interested. By the time I got around to it, they were grown men living their lives. A long-lost father didn't really rate. If I should end up a statistic, I'll be sorry I didn't work harder to build bridges."

"You have no other children? You never married again?" Wentworth broke one of his cardinal social rules, which was never to inquire about other people's personal lives, even when invited. Uncharacteristically, however, he felt a need for some sort of meaningful human connection, and the man beside him with his matter-of-fact calmness about their physical danger gave Wentworth an odd feeling of security.

"Serial girlfriends. Got one pregnant. She had an abortion. So no other kids that I know about."

It always surprised Wentworth how open Americans were to tell perfect strangers intimate details of their personal lives. It was so different from the British.

"I have two young sons myself," Wentworth said guardedly. "They go to Public School. It would be the same as a private preparatory college in the U.S. They board, of course, so I don't see much of them."

"You married?" Meadows had swivelled around on his stool to look at Wentworth directly.

"Yes, after a fashion. My wife and I tolerate each other would be the best way of putting it."

"Better than hating each other's guts." Meadows shrugged and took another gulp of his drink. "Mind if I give you a bit of advice?" he said. Wentworth nodded his head. "Spend time with those boys of yours before it's too late. They grow up awful fast."

The American emptied his glass, heaved himself up, and turned toward the elevator. "It's been nice talking to you, mister. I expect I'll see you around. There's no fucking place else we can go."

Wentworth was once again alone. He wasn't looking forward to going back to his room. It meant a long night alone with his thoughts. He had never given much thought to death, certainly not his own. The hellish situation in which he now found himself was forcing him to confront his own mortality. He'd never believed in an afterlife. As far as he was concerned, death meant oblivion, and the thought terrified him. He considered getting so drunk he would just pass out when he got to bed, but he was afraid of waking up in the horrors. His morning-after episodes were getting more frequent and traumatic.

It used to be he'd have a bad reaction after a night of drinking every couple of months. Now, it happened on a weekly basis. Wentworth just wanted to wake up one morning and discover that everything he was experiencing, running over the kid, being trapped in the middle of a civil war, all of it, was just a bad dream. Events were crowding in on him, suffocating him. He needed to see his two boys. It was through them that some part of himself would survive into the future. He was desperate for that validation. The hotel was becoming extremely claustrophobic. Wentworth wondered how much longer he could stick it out. He left his glass of whiskey half-finished and headed for his room.

If Wentworth was finding his stay at the Peninsula Hotel claustrophobic, the same could not be said of Lou Holt, at least as far as Josh Steinberg could tell. He was observing his friend revelling in a poker game with six other trapped guests.

"Full house, gentlemen, kings over tens, read 'em and weep."

There was a substantial pile of cash of different currencies in front of Holt. The night had been very good for him. Josh had quit playing an hour earlier, having lost two hundred dollars, considering that to be quite enough damage for one evening.

"Time for a bathroom break and a quick snack," Lou beamed. "Don't go anywhere, fellas, I'll be back shortly to give you a chance to get your revenge." He turned to Josh. "Order us a couple of sandwiches while I drain the snake."

"They made us a ham and Swiss. I asked for roast beef but they're all out," Josh said apologetically when Lou got back.

"Pickings are going to get slim all right," Lou said as he attacked his food. "They have several hundred staff and guests, and no deliveries."

"What will we do when the food runs out?" Josh asked anxiously.

"So long as they have beer, I'm not complaining."

"How can you be so adolescent, Lou?" Josh said angrily. "There are women with infants and young children trapped here."

"You need to live in the moment, Josh, and stop fretting about what you can't control," Lou said calmly. He put his hand on Josh's shoulder and looked him in the eye. "The folks running this hotel are no amateurs. They know exactly what provisions they have on hand. If this siege continues to drag on, I have no doubt they'll start rationing food, prioritising who gets what, and the likes of you and me, old son, will be relying on beer and chips."

It dawned on Josh that his friend was two steps ahead of him. "I'm sorry, Lou. You're right of course. I'm just freaked out by this whole thing."

"That's okay, pal. The trick is to focus on what you can control and forget the rest. Otherwise, you're just going to end up doing something stupid or giving yourself a one-way ticket to the funny farm. Me, for instance, I see an opportunity to fleece a few of my fellow guests at poker. Why don't you go chat up a couple of the young lovelies littered around this place and see if you can't get yourself laid? Nothing like a life-threatening situation to rev up the old sex drive. It's nature's way of preserving the species."

Sex was the furthest thing from Josh's mind, but he did feel a need for human interaction. He noticed an older woman seated in one of two armchairs separated by a coffee table in the atrium. She was writing in her journal.

"Do you mind if I join you?" he asked. She looked up at him, her gaze steady.

"Not at all, young man. Do I detect an East Coast accent?"

"Yes, ma'am. I'm from Boston."

"I'm from New York City myself. Manhattan, the Upper East Side."

The qualification did not surprise Josh. New Yorkers were like that. There was a certain element of snobbery to it. The woman was slim and well-coiffed. She wore a blue cotton dress which looked as if it had been custom fitted. There were diamond studs in her ears, and a simple silver necklace at her throat. Her fingers were unadorned. He guessed her age to be late fifties to early sixties. She did not immediately return her attention to her journal, which Josh took as an invitation to continue the conversation. As he sat down, he asked, "What brings you to Manila ma'am?"

"The name's Roberta, Roberta Ogilvy. I came to visit my father's grave. He was killed here in 1942. I was fifteen at the time. I haven't had the opportunity until now. I recently buried my husband after a long illness. Times were hard after the war. There just wasn't the money to make the trip. Then you get caught up in living your life. You know how it is." It was a lot of information. She trailed off, sounding almost apologetic.

"Josh Steinberg." He put out his hand, and she clasped it briefly. "It's perfectly understandable, Mrs Ogilvy. We're on the other side of the world over here, and air travel is expensive. I'm just sorry you've ended up making the visit in the middle of this mess. I hope it's not too distressing for you."

"When you get to my age, Mr Steinberg, your thoughts tend to dwell on the people in your life that have passed on. What happens in the here and now seems less important somehow. So no, I am not unduly worried."

"But you're not old, Roberta, I mean Mrs Ogilvy," Josh said, startled.

He was rewarded by an amused gleam in his companion's clear blue eyes. "I'm old enough to be your mother, young man, but I thank you for the compliment."

"I just got here a couple of weeks ago myself on a business assignment. I have a girlfriend, a local girl. I'm very worried about her," Josh blurted out. He didn't know why he'd made the confession to this perfect stranger. He paused, embarrassed.

"It's perfectly understandable to be concerned for those we love at a time like this."

Roberta's words, accepting and empathetic, were a balm to Josh's agitated state of mind. They were a sharp contrast to the harsh male pragmatism of Lou. There was a placid calmness about the older woman that invited confidences. Josh found himself telling her all about his time in Manila. He shared with her his confusion and the state of his emotions since arriving in the country, particularly when it came to Rita. He found tears coming to his eyes as he put into words his fears for her safety.

Roberta reached over and laid her hand on his arm. It was cool to the touch. He noticed her skin was toned and firm. His eyes strayed involuntarily to the curve of her breasts. He hastily collected himself.

"It's almost lunchtime. I've been bending your ear for an hour and more. I wonder would you like to get something to eat with me? I promise to stop treating you like an agony aunt."

"That would be delightful. If you give me a few minutes to go back to my room and freshen up, we could meet near the elevators in, say, twenty minutes?" She gave him a warm smile. He was surprised at how much pleasure that gave him.

When she reappeared half an hour later, Roberta had changed her dress to a lilac green, a little lower cut, and she was in high heels. He detected a faint smell of perfume as he escorted her to the restaurant. Belatedly, he thought he should have changed his own clothes or at least combed his hair, but the slacks and shirt were fresh on that morning, and he had remembered to shave. He caught sight of himself and the woman in the mirror behind the maître d' as they waited to be escorted to their table. They made quite the handsome couple. Roberta had a very erect posture, and he looked tanned and fit.

Lunch was a leisurely affair. The conversation meandered around a myriad of topics, from the profound to the banal. They split a bottle of wine between them, and under its influence, they found themselves sharing more intimate and personal confidences.

"George, my husband, was several years older than I. He was diagnosed five years ago with Lou Gehrig's disease. Amyotrophic lateral sclerosis is the official medical term for it. In the latter stages, my role became that of his nurse, or caregiver. I stopped thinking of myself as a wife. We had no children, you see, so it was largely left up to me to care for him."

Josh, who by this time had ended up telling Roberta the story of his life, listened attentively, his chin cupped in his hand.

"I felt at a loose end back in New York, and I made this trip as a way of regaining something of my own identity, I suppose." Roberta looked at her hands ruefully. "I wake up one morning to discover I am an old woman. Age crept up on me and I didn't notice. I was too wrapped up looking after George."

"Stop calling yourself old," Josh said firmly. "I don't think of you as old. You have more life and vivacity about you than any of the women I've dated back in the States, and you have a figure that would put a lot of them to shame."

She blushed. "And just how large is this field of women you are comparing me with, Josh? Am I talking to some sort of 20th-century Casanova?" She said it in a light, almost mocking tone.

"Don't make fun of me," Josh said defensively. "I've had a few relationships, but I'm not promiscuous, if that's what you're getting at."

She was instantly contrite. "Oh, I am sorry. It's just that it's been so long since I've been complimented by a man, and such a young man at that, I'm not sure how to respond."

Josh lent over impulsively and kissed her. "I've wanted to do that for the last hour and a half," he confessed. "If you want to slap my face, go ahead, but I don't regret it."

Roberta put her hand to her lips and gazed at him wonderingly. "I'm certainly not going to slap your face, but I do think you are a very fickle young man. Before lunch you were telling me how heartbroken you were that the local girl you were in love with had rejected you; now after lunch and a couple of glasses of wine you're making advances to me. How am I supposed to take this seriously?"

"I know I'm fickle, but the thing with Rita was just an infatuation. Talking with someone sane from home helped me to get my head straight. Rita is right. I'm just a guy who's paying for sex. Oh, they dress it up here as something else and you get caught up in the illusion, but these girls don't want to be doing this. Me and guys like me are just taking advantage of them. I wouldn't dream of carrying on like this back home. I'd think it was disgusting. But I am worried about her. That part of what I told you is true. But I'm not prepared to keep on taking advantage of her."

She was looking at him sharply. "So, you're going to distract yourself by trying to have a fling with an older woman, is that it?"

"That's not it at all, Roberta. I genuinely like you. I think you like me. We're caught up in this crazy situation. I'm just looking for a meaningful human connection in the middle of this insanity."

"And the kiss. Is that enough of a human connection for you, or were you looking to take this further?"

She sounded curious. He covered her hand with his own. She did not withdraw it.

"Well, you didn't recoil. Look, I didn't plan any of this. It just happened. I find you very attractive, Roberta." He took a deep breath. "I want to go to bed with you."

She smiled. "Well at least you didn't insult my intelligence by telling me you loved me, Josh. You are very handsome, I'll give you that." She stopped looking at him and shifted her gaze to survey the other guests in the dining room. "You're right, of course, that the situation is bizarre. Bizarre and dangerous. It's been a long time, years in fact, since I've experienced any form of physical intimacy. This might be my last opportunity. So why not? Yes, Josh, I'll go to bed with you. First, though, you had better order me a glass of brandy. I'm going to need a little more Dutch courage to go through with this."

There was a palpable frisson of sexual excitement as Roberta slowly sipped the brandy. Josh watched her, at once nervous and thrilled. In the end she pushed the glass away half-finished.

"I've had enough. I can't honestly say I even liked it. Shall we go to your room or mine?"

"Would you mind if we went to your room, Roberta?" Josh was bashful. "Mine isn't very presentable."

She smiled tolerantly. "What young man's is?"

They retired to her room. "Can you pull the curtains?" Roberta asked. "I'm just going to change in the bathroom. I won't be a moment."

Taking a negligee, she slipped into the bathroom. Josh did as he was asked, stripped down to his boxers and got under the covers. As he lay propped up on the pillows, he wondered what he had let himself in for. *What is she going to look like without her clothes? I hope it isn't going to be a turnoff.*

Roberta returned, her shape silhouetted by the bathroom light behind her. As she slipped into the bed, he noticed with relief that her bare arms were toned.

She must do yoga or work out or something.

As she embraced him with a fierce and hungry passion, any anxiety he might have had about his ability to perform vanished. It was as they lay in post-coital contentment that they heard a huge explosion outside. Josh, stark naked, ran to the window, pulled apart the heavy curtains and looked out.

"It's a tank!" he yelled. "They're shelling the building across the street."

Chapter Twenty-One

"For fuck's sake!" Bongo yelled. "The bastards have turned their tanks on us." He grabbed a grenade launcher propped against the wall of the apartment, raced over to the gaping hole where the window had been, and fired off a round at the turret of the lead tank. The explosion buffeted the massive vehicle, but it emerged undamaged. Bongo turned away in disgust.

"I don't know why I did that," he muttered. "It's just a waste of ammunition." The tank's main gun shifted to its left, preparing to fire again. "Sergeant, get the men off this floor." Bongo was already making for the door. "Take them down the stairs to the basement. They'll be safer there. I'm going to the roof to see if we can't do something about those fucking tanks with the mortar up there. Let's hope to God they have some shells left."

The gunner regarded Bongo impassively, a cigarette dangling from his mouth. "We have the shells, sure, lieutenant, but we can't use the mortar on that one down below."

"Why the fuck not?" Bongo was incredulous.

"The angle is too steep. We're ranged farther down the street, but this target is right below us. If we lob a mortar near vertical, it's as likely to land on us as your tank."

"Well, how do you propose we deal with the fucking thing before it blows us all to kingdom come?" Bongo barked in frustration.

"A well-aimed round from an RPG would do the job."

The entire building shuddered as another shell tore through it. Bongo flinched and staggered at the impact. The gunner, who was squatting low to the ground, seemed unfazed.

"And if we don't happen to have one of those lying around just now?" Bongo asked sarcastically. RPGs were the weapon of choice for Islamist or communist insurgents, not government troops who usually didn't have to face armour.

"Open the hatch and pop a grenade in." The gunner shrugged. "Tank itself will probably survive, but the crew will be turned into salsa."

"That's it, then," Bongo decided. "I'm going down to street level. When I send up a flare, you and your guys here—" He gestured toward the other two men squatted around the mortar. "—lay down covering fire while I try to cook that tank crew. Then try to find something with that fucking mortar you can hit."

The gunner regarded Bongo with a mixture of disbelief and renewed respect.

Two more rounds shook the building before Bongo reached the ground floor. The tank would swiftly reduce the apartments to rubble if not stopped. As he made his way down, Bongo briefly considered just abandoning his post and trying to run the government gauntlet surrounding Makati, but he quickly dismissed it from his mind. For one thing, there was a strong chance of his being captured or killed; for another, it would mean abandoning his men, and anyway, the fucking tank had begun to piss him off.

The scene that greeted him when he reached the lobby was grim. Several dead bodies were dumped unceremoniously in a corner, some still bleeding. Soldiers and residents lay moaning along another wall, faces gashed by shattered glass.

"I need a flare gun and a couple of grenades, quick," Bongo called out. A soldier with a makeshift bandage over one eye hurried over and pressed the items into his hands.

Bongo shoved the grenades into his pockets, raced for the foyer door, and plastered himself against the outside wall of the building. He shot the flare into the air and held his breath. A couple of seconds later, a hail of bullets rained down on the tank from the roof above.

Bongo crept along the wall. *If I step out on the street, I'll get mowed down by my own men,* he thought as he manoeuvred himself opposite the tank. Then he made a dash.

His first attempt to clamber onto the fuselage failed, his fingers clawing vainly, trying to find purchase. Bongo retreated several paces down the street, then turned and launched himself at the tank.

This time his momentum carried him up and he was able to swing himself onto the turret. He yanked open the hatch, pulled the pin on one of the grenades, and tossed it down on the startled, upturned face of one of the crew. Then he slammed the hatch shut and rolled off the tank, hitting the ground painfully with his shoulder.

He sprang to his feet and started running for the door of the apartment building. As he glanced back, he saw the hatch open again as one of the tankers inside tried to get rid of the grenade. A hail of bullets riddled the guy from above, and he fell back, still clutching it. An explosion and a burst of flame billowed from the open hatch. Bongo's sense of fierce elation was short-lived, however. Just as he reached the door, the building was rocked by a shell fired from another tank further down the street.

It's all been for nothing, Bongo thought despairingly. Just then, the second tank was hit by a mortar shell and exploded with a deafening roar. *I must buy that mortarman a drink.*

Bongo stumbled back into the building and leaned up against a wall to catch his breath. Captain Mendoza, catching sight of him, strode over.

"Nice work with those tanks, Lieutenant. It would have been all over with us if they had been allowed to continue the barrage."

"What are our orders going forward, Captain?" Bongo was too tired to acknowledge the compliment. Besides, he was aggravated that Mendoza, his commanding officer, had been little help he was putting his ass on the line.

"I just got off the line with headquarters. They're in serious negotiations with the government for a cessation of hostilities."

Bongo snorted his disbelief. "You wouldn't know it from what's being going on here for the last half hour."

Mendoza shrugged. "The government's just trying to improve their situation on the ground. Or it might have been a local commander trying to win a medal. Our orders are to continue to hold out here as best we can, or if our situation is no longer tenable, to fall back to another building in the vicinity."

"What are we supposed to use for ammunition, sir?" was Bongo's reply.

Our company has been torn to shreds and these clowns at HQ think we're going to be able to waltz in and occupy another building under the noses of the government troops, with their armour and their fucking tanks.

"They're going to try to resupply us under cover of darkness tonight. We just have to hang tough. Every hour we don't concede works in our favour, Bongo." Alejandro Mendoza was almost pleading with him.

"Can we at least ask for a ceasefire for an hour or so to get rid of the dead? That lot—" Bongo gestured with his thumb in the direction of the bodies. "—are beginning to smell. Anyway, I'm sure the Aquino people will want to collect their own guys from the street, not to mention their barbecued tank crew. We should also ask to evacuate the injured."

Mendoza nodded grimly. "I'll send someone out under a flag of truce. It can't hurt to ask."

Thirty minutes later, a truce of two hours was agreed upon. A couple of trucks pulled up in the street outside, having weaved their way around the wreckage of the tanks and lumps of masonry from the shattered building. The able-bodied men still left ferried the bodies onto one truck, and the wounded on makeshift stretchers to the other.

Mendoza approached Bongo as he was helping one of his men sling a moaning man onto a stretcher. "Lieutenant, let someone else do that. I have another assignment for you."

Sounds ominous, Bongo thought.

"While the ceasefire is in force, I need you to do a reconnaissance of the nearby buildings in case we have to pull back. We agreed we'd stop shooting. It doesn't mean we can't have a look around. Change into some civilian clothes. The locals will have got wind of the ceasefire and a few of them will have put their noses out in the street to see what's going on. You can blend in."

Once again, Bongo felt a surge of irritation with his commanding officer. *No likelihood of putting yourself in harm's way,* he thought contemptuously.

"Focus on an expensive apartment complex, if you can. A lot of them will belong to one or other of the oligarch families. They won't be taking kindly to having some of their prime real estate blown to kingdom come. It'll put more pressure on the government to come to terms with us." Mendoza smiled knowingly.

The assets of the wealthy families are valuable and to be protected. Our lives, the lives of the ordinary Filipinos, are cheap.

"Whatever you say, Captain." He gave a deliberately sloppy salute and headed off to ransack one of the empty apartments for civilian clothes.

Josh was in his hotel room grabbing clothes, toiletries, and a pillow and blanket off his bed. The tank assault on the building opposite had caused hotel management to instruct all guests to gather their essentials and make their way to the grand ballroom for safety. As he gathered up his things, he was filled with anxiety and post-coital remorse for his tryst with Roberta Ogilvy.

I must have been crazy and now I'm not even going to be able to avoid the woman. We're all going to be one big happy family in that fucking ballroom. Joshua Steinberg, what a dipshit you are.

He thought about Rita, and his feelings alternated between guilt and defiance. He had cheated on her. But what did that even mean? She was the one who had dumped him. He was a free man without commitments.

That was the problem, though. He did feel committed to her.

So, she blows you off and you react by thinking with your dick. And Roberta, what about her? Whatever he might have said or even momentarily felt during their encounter, in the end, it was just a roll in the hay. Roberta, however, might not see it that way. He replayed in his head his protestations of love and winced.

He crammed the last of his belongings into his satchel and took a last look around the room. *Time to face the music,* Josh thought as he headed for the stairs.

The scene that greeted him when he reached the ballroom was a melee of disorganised bodies and the grating sound of screaming infants. Frantic hotel staff were alternately yelling instructions or being berated by agitated guests.

Josh cast about frantically, with the dual purpose of avoiding Roberta Ogilvy and connecting with Lou Holt. Eventually he saw his friend, his chair leaned back against a wall, feet splayed out in front of him, wolfing yet another sandwich from a Styrofoam box on his lap, a beer in one hand.

"Do you ever stop eating?" Josh said as he settled down beside him.

"I'd chow down on whatever's on offer, buddy. It's going to be slim pickings around here before very long. But they've assured me they're unlikely to run out of beer or pizza. With those essential food groups, I'm good to go for the duration." Lou belched contentedly.

"How long do you think they can keep us here?" Josh said. "I need to see Rita."

"I wouldn't sweat it. We're not going anywhere for a while. Besides, from what you've told me, it's not even clear she wants to see you." Lou looked around. "Sanitation is going to be a problem. There are long lines for the bathrooms as it is, and not everyone has arrived yet. As for keeping yourself clean—" He snorted. "—it's going to get pretty aromatic around here before long."

From the corner of his eye, Josh saw Roberta enter the ballroom. He pressed himself against the wall and hurriedly twisted his body toward Lou.

"Christ, there she is. Please let her not come in this direction."

"Who?" Lou asked, startled.

"The woman in the green dress who just came in," Josh said hoarsely.

Lou squinted at the ballroom entrance. "The old broad with the long grey hair? What about her?"

Josh looked at Lou with an agonised expression. "I did a foolish thing, Lou."

He looked at Josh, and his slowly dawning comprehension was mixed with incredulity. "Well, you sly dog, Steinberg." He chortled loudly.

"For God's sake, Lou don't draw attention to us," Josh implored.

"Okay, okay," Lou said, stifling his mirth. "Here you've been bleating on about Rita this and Rita that, and I love Rita, and meantime you've been porking someone old enough to be your mother. At least tell me you were drunk at the time."

"She's a nice woman, Lou, and we made a connection. It's just that I don't want her to get the idea there's any future in it."

"You mean you're not signed up for quiet moonlight walks together, just you, her, and the Zimmer frame?" Lou was wiping his eyes, tears of laughter glistening.

"You're being a complete asshole, you know that?" Josh said angrily.

"Sorry, pal. Just couldn't help myself." Lou shook his head and became serious. "For a start, this isn't high school, buddy. You're not some hormone-stricken teenager the day after the school prom. The old dame—"

"Her name is Roberta."

"Roberta then, doesn't look like a bunny boiler to me, though you never can tell. You need to man up and tell her the score if you have to. Anyway, it may not come to that. She may just have regarded you as a nice piece of meat to distract her from our current situation. Of course, that would have been 'cuz she hadn't laid eyes on yours truly." Lou preened. "What you do now is get up off your fat ass and go over there and ask her if she needs help with anything. Take it from there. You can use me as an excuse if you need to get away. Tell her I'm having some sort of panic attack."

"Thanks, Lou," Josh said gratefully as he clambered to his feet. "Do me a favour, though. Stop wolfing that sandwich. Doesn't square with a guy on the edge somehow."

"If you insist," Lou grumbled, putting the remainder of his sandwich back in the box. "The things I do for friendship."

"Hi Roberta, I'm glad you made it down here safely," Josh said awkwardly as he came up beside her.

"Yes, it is fortunate, seeing as my gallant knight errant left me to fend for myself," Roberta replied cooly. Josh blushed. "Oh, for heaven's sake, Josh, can't you see I'm just teasing you? I'm well used to being self-sufficient. I noticed you sitting with another young man as I came in. Is he a friend of yours?" Roberta said this in a light conversational tone that Josh found disconcerting.

You'd hardly think that we were rolling around in bed together less than an hour ago, he thought, nonplussed. "He's a colleague," he said, glancing back. "Would you care to join us?" He didn't know what else to say.

"I think I'll take a turn around the room before I decide where to park myself." Roberta's eyes were taking in the human drama unfolding on the floor of the grand ballroom as she spoke.

"About what happened between us earlier," Josh began haltingly.

She shot him an annoyed glance. "I hardly think this is a suitable venue to have a discussion about that," she said sharply.

"You're right, no, of course not," he stammered.

"Why don't you go back to your friend. We can reconnect at some later point." She gestured at the room. "It's not as though either of us are going anywhere, after all."

"Okay. Just remember I'm around if you need me for anything." Josh felt a curious mixture of relief and resentment at being so summarily dismissed. Roberta smiled briefly at him before turning to pick her way through the various groups of people.

Across the ballroom, Philip Wentworth endured the stench of a soiled diaper. It clearly belonged to one of two screaming children in the family next to him. He felt the bile rising in his throat and wanted to vomit. *I'm not going to be able to endure this hellhole for very long,* he thought desperately.

The whole situation was surreal, nightmarish. He kept hoping it was just an alcohol-fuelled hallucination, but the nauseating smell disabused him of that notion. His primary concern was for his safety. The situation just kept deteriorating, and he had no sense that anyone was doing anything about it. He looked around. Too many people, not enough food, and no semblance of authority or discipline. At some point soon it was going to degenerate to the law of the jungle in the bloody ballroom, and he was not particularly well equipped for that scenario.

How in God's name am I going to get out of here? The giant chandelier shook each time a shell slammed into the building opposite and Wentworth started fearfully at each impact. *It's like something from fucking Phantom of the Opera.*

"Can you not keep that bloody child quiet?" he shouted at the frantic mother beside him. "And deal with the snot rags of shit while you're about it." People around him reacted with dismay at his outburst, but he could have cared less. He took out a cigar and lit it. The cigar smoke might do something to lessen the awful smell. The young mother, humiliated, dragged her two children in the direction of the bathrooms.

That should keep her busy for an hour or so, thought Wentworth, having seen the lines as he came into the ballroom. He had emptied the contents of the minibar before leaving his room, and now poured two small bottles of whiskey into a tumbler, downing the contents in a single gulp.

Wentworth pondered his options. He had no passport and no money. What he did have was a Rolex watch that would easily fetch 10k Sterling were he in London, and a Van Cleef and Arpels signet ring worth maybe 5k. If he could just get out of the fucking hotel, he could raise some decent cash on the black market, even if he had to let the two pieces go for a discount. Maybe then he could find a fisherman at the port who would ferry him to Hong Kong without asking too many questions. Hong Kong was British. He could fast talk his way to a BA flight home from there.

What he really needed was a local to help him leave the hotel and escape from Makati. He would need to ask around among the hotel staff. Filipinos were lazy and untrustworthy, but he didn't have much of a choice. Right now, though, he wanted something to eat, and above all, more alcohol—a lot more.

He foraged around in his wallet to see what cash he had left—10,000 pesos, 200 sterling, 500 dollars. For the locals this represented a small fortune, but Wentworth knew that as the situation dragged on, his money would be less and less useful.

He surveyed the members of the hotel staff as they mingled among the guests, picking up garbage, fielding queries, distributing food and water. Wentworth had a nose for people on the make. It didn't matter the nationality, it was something about the body language, the way they looked at people. Eventually, his gaze landed on an older-looking Filipino who was filling a trash bag with discarded Styrofoam lunch boxes. He had a disinterested look about him. Wentworth made his move and sidled up to his mark.

"Mind if I give these to you?" Wentworth dropped the two mini whiskey bottles into the trash bag. Folded between the fingers of his hand was a $20 bill. The man's eyes narrowed. "Last of my whiskey, I'm afraid. I don't suppose you know how I could lay my hands on a decent bottle of scotch?"

"I'm sorry, sir, we have suspended bar service." The man had not taken his eyes off the money.

"I know that. All the same, if you could lay hands on a bottle, there'd be another $100 in it for you."

He snatched the $20 from between Wentworth's fingers. "I'll see what I can do, sir."

Greedy bastard, Wentworth thought. *We'll see how he does and then find out if he's good for anything else.*

Twenty minutes later, the staff member was back. Concealed in a large white dinner napkin was a bottle of Scotch. Furtively, the alcohol was swapped for the money. Wentworth slipped the bottle into his rucksack.

"I need to get out of here… Marco," Wentworth said, shooting a quick glance at the man's nametag. "The name's Wentworth, by the way. Do you think you could get me away from Makati?"

"It's far too dangerous, sir. People have already died in the streets. You're much safer here."

"You don't understand," Wentworth improvised quickly. "My daughter is critically ill back home in England. I desperately need to get back."

Marco's eyes darted quickly to the holdall and then returned to look at Wentworth critically.

Fuck, he's probably thinking a frantic father doesn't go round bribing the help to get him bottles of whiskey.

"I'm at my wits end, my nerves are shot. I'll make it worth your while."

Marco continued to shake his head.

"Listen, a thousand bucks to get me out of here. Five hundred now, five hundred when you drop me at the port."

The size of his offer brought about a change in Marco's attitude. Wentworth could always recognise the glint of greed in other men's eyes.

"My brother has a truck. I could ask him if he would help, but it is very dangerous."

Did Marco believe his story? It didn't matter whether he did or not. Wentworth had successfully laid the bait. His fish was hooked. "When will you know?"

Marco rubbed his chin thoughtfully. "My shift finishes in a couple of hours. I will try to contact him then."

"Good man. I'm extremely grateful." Wentworth pressed another $20 into Marco's hand. "Let me know as soon as you find anything out."

Josh was woken from a deep slumber by the sharp point of a woman's shoe prodding his calf. He peered up bleary-eyed to see Roberta Ogilvy looming over him.

"We should have our chat, Josh, to clear the air."

"What, now?" Josh said, startled. He glanced at his watch. "It's after eleven o'clock, Roberta, for Chrissake. Most people are asleep."

"Exactly." Roberta was unperturbed. "We might be afforded a little bit of privacy. I don't particularly want an alert audience for what we're going to discuss, do you?"

"Oh, alright then." He hauled himself to his feet.

"There's a small unoccupied space over there against the far wall. It looks like the people closest to it are asleep," Roberta said.

They picked their way over prone bodies until they found themselves propped side by side against the wall.

"Have you ever seen the play *The Night of the Iguana*, Josh?"

"What sort of a dumbass question is that, Roberta? And no, I haven't seen the fucking play." Josh was now in a thoroughly bad mood. "You stiff me this morning when I was only trying to be polite, and now you wake me up in the middle of the night to play some sort of quiz show game." He turned to face her angrily. She made no effort to return his gaze.

"It's a play by Tennessee Williams. One of the principal characters is a disgraced American clergyman who makes a living as a guide for bus tours, made up largely of women visiting Mexico. He preys on his clients sexually. To soften them up, as it were, to loosen their inhibitions, he makes a point of taking them past scenes of squalor on the way to their hotel."

"And that's what you're saying I did, Roberta? Took advantage of your vulnerability? You're saying I'm some sort of pervert? Why don't you just come out and say it instead of dressing it up in New Yorkish Upper East Side psychobabble?" He grabbed her arm.

"Let go of me Josh, you're hurting me." She twisted to get free of him.

He relinquished his grip immediately. "I'm sorry," he said gruffly. "For grabbing your arm, I mean. Not for what I just said. It's incredible you can think of me like that."

She blushed and lost something of her poise. "Oh Josh, I didn't mean to imply... I'm not expressing myself very well." Roberta said it more to herself than to him. "The point I wanted to make was that being placed in a setting which shocks one's sensibilities makes one more prone to act out of character. I'm not suggesting you single-handedly manufactured this coup for the purpose of seducing me. That would be absurd. And no, I don't think you're like the reverend Larry Shannon, that's the character's name. Except maybe that you're a confused soul like he is." Josh continued to regard her with hurt suspicion.

"In my world it's very hard to talk directly about feelings," she continued. "We often deflect by talking about the emotions of characters in a play or an opera. It's just a way of communicating without really having to bare your soul. I got caught up in a situation, we both did, and I acted out. I'm frightened I'm not going to get out of here alive. You were a nice young boy who seemed to take an interest in me, and I needed an escape. I thought I could recapture a sense of youth and vitality. But all it's done is overwhelm me with how desperately I miss my husband." She began to sob.

Oblivious to everyone around them, he pulled her to him and held her. "Please don't cry, Roberta. We'll come out of this okay,

I'm sure we will. We had a moment, it was a very nice moment, but yes, it's not who either of us are, or what we really want. Look at my mate Lou Holt over there." Gently, he turned her face to look a little way down the ballroom.

"If he's not eating, he's gambling. First it was cards, now see, he's playing craps. He's acting out. Everyone in this room is, one way or another. Let's try and be kind to ourselves and to each other. It's the only way we're going to get through this hellish situation."

"I take it back, Joshua," Roberta said as she dried her eyes. "You're not naïve at all. It turns out you're a very sensible young man."

Chapter Twenty-Two

Bongo Cruz surveyed the team of men he had assembled for his mission with scepticism. It was the second night after the ceasefire, which had successfully led to the removal of the dead and wounded from the combat zone. Bongo, as ordered, had taken advantage of the cessation of hostilities to reconnoitre other buildings in the vicinity. Government troops were on the streets in numbers but surprisingly had not posted guards in any of the apartment complexes themselves.

Bongo had zeroed in on a building two doors down, which was set back a bit from the street with a narrow sweeping drive. A large ornamental stone mound with carved swans shielded its entrance, so a direct frontal assault on the building was not possible. Identifying the target was one thing, but securing it would be quite another. Three of his best men were dead and half a dozen others were wounded, two with injuries severe enough to require evacuation during the ceasefire.

The ten men who remained were incredibly young. None of were out of their teens, and a couple looked as if they hadn't started to shave. Bongo had serious doubts about how they would perform in a firefight. The best strategy by far would be to avoid one entirely. It was Alejandro Mendoza's job to create a diversion, and Bongo prayed it would be a good one. They had deliberately tried to dial down the level of hostilities over the last forty-eight hours to cause their opponents to settle into a routine and seemingly, it had worked. The government troops relaxed at their guard posts, chatting to each other, smoking the odd cigarette.

"Five minutes to go-time," Bongo told his nervous youngsters.

One had his nails bitten down almost to the quick and was even now gnawing at them anxiously. Another, busy combing his hair, appeared to be admiring himself in a full-length mirror in the lobby, which had miraculously survived the siege so far.

Where does he think he's going? Bongo thought incredulously. *On a date?*

Right at the stroke of 2 a.m. Mendoza cut loose. Flares fired from their gutted bolt-hole illuminated the street below, shrouding the whole area in smoke. The rattle of automatic rifles sent the government troops scurrying for cover as they began to return a ragged, ill-aimed fire.

"Move. Stay low!" Bongo yelled as he led his men, ducking and weaving to run the gauntlet the few hundred yards to their objective. Two loyalist soldiers, seeing the manoeuvre, attempted to redirect their fire in his direction. He mowed them down with a couple of short, staccato bursts from his M14.

He shot a quick glance behind him to see how the others were faring. "Keep your fucking heads down!"

Too late. The boy at the rear of the group, running upright and clearly visible under the light of a streetlamp, clutched at his neck as a fountain of blood burst through his fingers.

"Stupid fucker," Bongo cursed.

An officer from the opposing side, seeing the rebels making a break for it and divining their goal, screamed at his men to block their path. Six of them formed ranks, three standing, three kneeling, and started to lay down a withering hail of fire.

"Take cover!" Bongo screamed. "Hand grenades now! Take the bastards out before they reinforce or we're finished!"

He hit the ground as bullets whistled over his head. He heard screams behind him. He lobbed a grenade at the six men in front of him as two more were lobbed from behind him.

The aim was good. His opponents were shredded.

"Now!" Bongo yelled. "Run for it. We're almost there."

A last adrenaline-fuelled rush got them to the lobby of the building. Seven of them had made it. Bongo looked back on the street. Two of his men were clearly dead and a third lay moaning, covered in blood.

"Shouldn't we try to get Miguel?" one survivor asked anxiously.

"And get ourselves killed and him too in the bargain? Fuck, no. I need four of you on an upper floor, say level seven, to cover the street." He gestured at the two men standing closest to him. "You two stay here with me."

Now that Bongo's squad had cleared a path to the building, they could cover the front approach for others to follow. "Where's the radio?" he said. "I need to let Captain Mendoza know we're in. We need to reinforce this place fast before the bastards have a chance to get their act together."

The next twenty minutes were frantic, with tense flurries of gunfire as the rebels evacuated their bombed-out building and relocated to the relatively unscathed apartment block a few doors down.

Once safely entrenched, Alejandro Mendoza and Bongo Cruz took advantage of a lull in the fighting to each smoke a cigar.

"Our friends seem to have gone quiet all of a sudden," Bongo remarked.

"They're waiting for orders. There isn't going to be much appetite for flattening another luxury high-rise belonging to one of the oligarch families."

"So, what do you think they'll do?"

Mendoza dropped the stub of his cigar and ground it into the polished floor with his foot. "Sneak attack, probably. They're going prioritise the integrity of the building over their soldiers' lives."

Bongo shrugged. "Suits us. It sucks for the poor bastards who'll make the assault."

Mendoza considered Bongo's analysis. "Join the guys you sent upstairs. Make sure they stay alert. I'll keep watch down here.

They'll make some sort of effort to dislodge us soon enough. They won't want us digging in."

Bongo nodded and moved toward the elevator, pleased that Mendoza was finally taking a more hands-on role in the operation.

The renewed bout of gunfire from the hotel's opposite side had completely unnerved Philip Wentworth. A paroxysm of panic combined with a crushing sense of claustrophobia overcame him. All he wanted was to get away from Manila and the godforsaken Peninsula Hotel.

This was the night he was supposed to make a break for it. He waited in the little office next to the hotel's service entrance with the waiter, whom he had bribed to organise his getaway as the man had an agitated discussion over the phone.

"My cousin does not want to make the run tonight. He says it's too dangerous."

Wentworth leaned up against the wall, hyperventilating. "Fuck that. I have to get out of this place, I just have to. Tell your cousin I'll double whatever you told him I'd pay him."

The waiter's eyes glittered with greed. There was a further heated exchange with the man on the other end of the line. "He says he'll wait to see if there's a lull in the shooting. You'll need to meet him out on the street, though. He's not going to risk pulling up to the side entrance and hanging about."

Wentworth felt at wit's end, his fear vying with the overwhelming urge to flee. Finally he said, "Screw it, okay. Tell him to wave a white cloth out the window as he's about to pull by. I'll be out there to meet him. What do we do now?"

"We wait," the man said.

After some fits and starts, the gunfire finally died down. It would be another half hour before the driver decided to make his move.

"What the fuck is he waiting for?" Wentworth kept whispering to his companion as the minutes ticked by. "We'll miss our opportunity."

At last, the van appeared, turning a street corner and driving slowly along Ayala Avenue. The driver was shaking a small towel out his window.

"Go, go now. What are you waiting for?" The waiter pushed Wentworth out from the doorway and he began a frightened, stumbling run toward the van.

From his seventh-floor window, Bongo Cruz saw the movement below. It took him a moment, but he recognised the ungainly figure of Philip Wentworth as he passed under one of the few streetlights that hadn't been shot out in the street battles. Bongo paused for a split second to think.

It's a pity to lose all that money, but blood is thicker than water after all. This one's for you, Cuz.

He took careful aim and shot Philip Wentworth through the head. The Englishman collapsed in a heap a few feet from the waiting van, which quickly sped off down the street.

The soldier at the window alongside Bongo was startled. "What did you do that for, Lieutenant? The man's not in uniform. He's a civilian for God's sake."

"I saw the glint of a revolver in his hand. These government bastards are trying a sneak attack. They've put some of their guys in street clothes to catch us off guard. That one won't be troubling us though." Bongo held his breath.

The soldier accepted the lie. "Well spotted, Lieutenant. I would have missed that."

Angel read about the death of Wentworth while sipping a cool lemonade on the deck of a 100-foot luxury yacht moored in Manila Bay. The newspaper didn't name him, but he was described as a middle-aged English businessman who had recently been involved in a traffic accident in which there had been a fatality. She was not particularly affected by the news except to feel a certain relief that it was unlikely now she would have to testify in any court proceedings.

The yacht, called *Final Fling,* was owned by her latest patron, an elderly New Zealander she had picked up in the bar of the Shangri La Hotel. He was old, in his mid-eighties, even older than her grandfather. He was so grateful she had agreed to go to bed with him that he had hired her for the entire time he was in Manila. It was supposed to be a month, but Angel had her doubts he would last that long so she insisted he pay half up front. As a client, he was pretty undemanding. Once she had overcome her initial revulsion at being pawed over by a wrinkled old cadaver, it had turned out to be a pretty easy assignment. He rose late and napped in the afternoon. That was what he was doing as she read the newspaper.

It was just the two of them on the yacht, albeit attended by a crew of twelve which included a chef, a waiter, a housemaid, and nine others to sail the vessel, although it had yet to leave its mooring while she was on board.

Angel was expected to join him for all his meals, which were served in a formal dining area with her at one end of the table and him at the other. Meals were eaten in total silence and took forever because he ate slowly and deliberately, chewing each morsel thoroughly before swallowing. She had initially tried to read a magazine to pass the time, only to be admonished for showing such bad manners at the table.

She mused idly about cajoling the old man into marrying her, but she doubted it would stick. He was effectively impotent, and there were photographs of what she took to be his extended family dotted around the yacht. On the whole, though, Angel was not displeased with her lot. As long as she kept her looks, there would always be some man or other to pay for the pleasure of her company. If she was careful and managed to put something away for herself, she might even be able to buy a bar and run a few girls as a mama-san herself. In any event, she was a survivor.

Chapter Twenty-Three

Josh was woken by an urge to use the bathroom. His limbs ached from lying on the ballroom floor. The blanket did little to pad the unyielding tile. He glanced at Lou beside him, flat on his back and snoring like a walrus.

Josh was surprised to find he had to line up to exit the ballroom. Until now, the guests had entered and left as they wished, so long as they stayed on the lower level. The hotel security personnel seemed a lot more on edge. Guests were shepherded to the bathrooms in single file and returned the same way. Those attempting to wander off were firmly instructed to return to the line. The round trip took a full thirty minutes. When he returned, Lou was awake, sitting cross-legged and happily smoking a cigar.

"Why the flap all of a sudden?" Josh asked as he slid down beside his friend.

"Some numb-nuts guest got himself shot in the early hours trying to get away from here. A Limey by all accounts, so they say. Management wants to keep a closer eye on us. They don't want a repeat performance. Not good for the brand image to have guests being potted by overenthusiastic snipers. But that's not the most upsetting thing."

"It isn't?" Josh asked with foreboding.

"Not by a long shot. This, old son—" Lou waved the cigar under Josh's nose. "—is the last Cohiba Cuban in the place. I had to slip the bartender 20 bucks to lay hands on it."

"You're incorrigible, Lou," Josh said, relieved in spite of himself.

"It's going to get pretty Third World here shortly with all these people crowded into a confined space," Lou said, becoming serious.

"Have you heard anything else about how long this will go on?" Josh asked as he tried to get comfortable.

"The staff I've talked to think the government and the rebels are close to a deal, but that may just be wishful thinking."

As Josh ran his gaze around the crowded ballroom, the strain on the other trapped guests was visible, particularly in their physical appearance. It was hard to associate the badly groomed, dishevelled bodies with the stylish, coiffed patrons of just a few days earlier.

"How am I going to keep myself from going crazy?" Josh put his head in his hands.

Lou pulled a deck of cards from the breast pocket of his shirt. "You know how to play gin?"

"No." Josh looked up.

"Here's your opportunity to learn a valuable life skill then," Lou said cheerfully. "You cut; I'll deal."

Josh and Lou had been playing for about an hour when their attention was drawn to an altercation in a corner of the ballroom a few hundred feet away. A young woman was trying to calm a hysterical infant who was screaming at the top of its lungs. The two older siblings were adding to the commotion by tugging at the mother and complaining, one that he was hungry and the other that she needed the bathroom. She was being berated by a burly man in his thirties who, along with his equally heavily built companion, was occupying a space next to hers. They both had shaved heads, no necks, and bulging biceps. To Josh, they looked like body builder types on steroids.

"Can't you shut that little shit up, lady?" one said.

The distraught mother spoke over her shoulder as she desperately tried to sooth the baby who now seemed to be hyperventilating. "I'm sorry, sir, I really am. My husband is trapped on the other side of the city and I'm here on my own with the three children. They're tired and frightened."

"I don't care where your asswipe of a husband is, lady. You have two minutes to get that kid to zip it or I'll do it for you, you dumb bitch."

Crowded though the room was, the people closest to the confrontation shrank back, creating a space around the woman, the children, and her roid rage assailant. Josh eyed the scene nervously.

Lou however, with a speed and agility which belied his bulk, was already on his feet and bulldozed his way over to stand protectively in front of the frightened woman and her terrified children.

"That's no way to talk to a lady cowboy. I think you owe her an apology," Lou said, smiling affably.

"What the fuck business is it of yours?" The man bunched his fists and made as though to swing a punch. He never made it.

Lou, with a smile still on his face, headbutted him, smashing his nose and brutally kneeing him in the groin at the same time. The man fell to his knees. Lou clasped his hands, bringing them down with full force on the back of his victim's neck and the man collapsed in a heap. Lou brought his foot down on the side of his hapless adversary's skull. He lay motionless, a pool of blood gathering around his head. The savagery of the encounter, coupled with its speed, left the onlookers stunned.

The downed man's companion pulled a hunting knife from a pocket of his cargo pants and lunged for Lou with a bellow of rage. Lou managed to twist away, avoiding the knife, and stuck out his leg in hopes of tripping this new opponent, but the man sprang back and readied himself for another attack.

Lou bent quickly to grab a rain jacket belonging to one of the bystanders and wrapped it around one arm never taking his eyes off the knife. "So what's the story with you pal?" he said conversationally. "Was he the appetiser and you're the main course, or are you just dessert?

The knife flashed again, this time missing the side of Lou's face by a fraction of an inch. The reflexes of both men were lightning-quick. They circled each other warily, Lou recoiling each time the knife sliced through the air.

Josh looked on, his heart in his mouth for his friend. *He can only dodge that knife for so long.* Just as he thought it, Lou, instead of avoiding the knife thrust, parried it with his protected arm, and stepping in, delivered a karate chop to his opponent's Adam's apple.

The man staggered back, dropping the knife as onlookers rushed in and grabbed him, wrestling him into submission. Lou unwrapped the protective garment from his arm and looked around apologetically for its owner.

"Sorry your coat is shredded buddy," Lou said, handing it back to an elderly gentleman who was eyeing him warily. "Steinberg!" he yelled over his shoulder. "Move your skinny ass and make room where you are for these nice people."

Lou smiled affably at the bewildered young woman. "Why don't you come over yonder near us, ma'am? A better class of neighbourhood, no offence to present company. Cute kid." He contorted his face into a stupid grin and blew a raspberry at the baby who was now watching him mesmerised.

The news that the siege was ending broke later that afternoon. Josh was trying unsuccessfully to nap, the blanket still completely useless as padding against the marble floor of the ballroom. He was roused by ragged cheering and applause.

"What's going on?" he asked Lou groggily.

Lou was exuberant. "The government and the rebels have done a deal. The rebels have agreed to a truce. A convoy of buses will evacuate us."

"Thank the living God," Josh said fervently. "Where will we be evacuated to?"

"Who cares?" Lou shrugged. "Out of this hellhole, anyway. I'm sure you could go straight to the airport if you wanted."

Josh shook his head. "You know I can't do that, Lou. Not without seeing Rita again. Will you leave?"

Lou was shocked. "What, and give up a very comfortable lifestyle because of this little local dust-up? You must be kidding me."

"Is that what you're calling this?" Josh looked at him in astonishment. "There are scores of people dead, and God knows how many wounded."

"Including that poor sod from last night," Lou said ruefully. "If he'd just hung tight a few more hours." He sighed and shrugged. "Still, that's how fickle life is."

Lou registered Josh's look of disbelief and bristled. "Listen, sunshine, you've only been here a short while, and it's obvious you can't wait to get back Stateside. Okay, sure, you've got your foot caught in the door, but once you've salved your conscience, you're out of here. For me, it's different. I've made a life for myself in the Philippines. There's nothing back in the States for me."

His eyes, which had been boring into Josh's while speaking, suddenly flickered and he grunted. "That one-night stand of yours is heading in our direction, obviously looking for you, pal. I'm not running interference for you this time, Josh. You're on your own." Lou clambered to his feet, turned his back on his friend, and headed for one of the side entrances.

Josh rose to greet Roberta and kissed her awkwardly on the cheek. "You've heard the news?"

She smiled and nodded. "Yes. The buses will leave for the airport in a couple of hours. I'm hoping to get a flight out tonight. Will you be staying on?" She looked at him quizzically.

"Yes, I think so. If just for a little while. I need to sort out what's up with the job and then there's…"

"I know. The young girl you've been seeing." She regarded his obvious discomfiture with sympathy.

"I don't know that I can leave just like that," he said, turning red.

"It's important to treat a meaningful relationship with respect," she agreed gravely.

He looked at her uncertainly, wondering if she was mocking him. "I'm sure to be back Stateside in a couple of months. Maybe we could connect?" he ventured.

"I don't know what purpose that would serve, Josh." She looked resolute, and any fleeting thoughts he harboured of renewing the tryst on a no-strings-attached basis vanished as rapidly as the impulse had come into his head. "Oh, the physical attraction is still there," she assured him. "I'll give you that. But that's not enough for me, not nearly enough."

"So, this is it then?" Suddenly he felt very sad.

"I'm rather afraid it is, Josh," she smiled kindly. "Still, what is it they say in that old Humphrey Bogart movie? We'll always have Manila."

Impulsively, he reached out and hugged her to him tight. She lingered in his arms for a few moments and then gently pushed away. "Goodbye, Josh."

She was gone.

Chapter Twenty-Four

"It's over." Alejandro Mendoza walked briskly over to where Bongo Cruz was sitting, propped up against a wall on the ground floor of their recently secured apartment building, sipping a lukewarm coffee. He squatted down beside him.

"We have orders to ready the men and march under arms, back to Fort Bonifacio. All units to depart simultaneously from their positions in Makati at 8 a.m."

"What are the terms?" Bongo asked anxiously.

"We surrender our weapons at the fort. The government agrees to treat us humanely, whatever that might mean." His commander was nonchalant.

"That's all very well, Mendoza, but are we going to be brought up on charges?" Bongo was worried about the two soldiers he had gunned down at the start of the coup.

Mendoza did not seem too concerned. "If past practice is anything to go by, there's not likely to be much fallout. Besides, Aquino is in a world of hurt over this. Her own vice president refused to condemn our insurrection, and the Nacionalista Party bigwigs are providing us with political cover. They're saying we had legitimate grievances while not going so far as to condone our actions. Our beloved president is being crucified in the press for involving the Americans. Her people are going to want to sweep this under the carpet as quickly as possible. Show trials are the last thing they need."

Bongo only felt partially reassured. He was of two minds between following orders and going on the run. He needed to talk to his father, who would be a better judge of the risks he faced than that blowhard Alejandro Mendoza.

"I'll let my guys know what's up," Bongo said, rising to his feet. It gave him an excuse to get away from his commander and place a phone call to his father. He went up a couple of floors, picked an apartment at random, and kicked the door in. He made a quick reconnaissance, finding the place empty.

There was a phone in the bedroom. He picked it up and heard a dial tone. There would have been no chance of that in the bombed-out shell of a building they had just evacuated. Bongo looked at his watch. It was just after 6 a.m. Too bad. He swiftly dialled the number and waited. It rang and rang. Eventually, his groggy father answered.

"Cruz here. Who is this calling?"

"It's me, Tatay. Have you heard? We've surrendered. Orders are to march back to our barracks. What do you think I should do? Is it safe for me do you think?"

"Are you asking me if the government troops will renege on the deal and shoot the lot of you? How should I know, Bongo?"

The old fool is going senile, Bongo thought angrily.

"No, I mean for me personally, Tatay. I'm worried if there will be fallout from the fracas I told you about." He needed to be circumspect in case his parents' phone was bugged.

"Oh yes, that." There was a pause. When his father finally answered, Bongo was relieved to hear the shrewd, confident tone was back in the old man's voice. It reassured him. "The tide is going out for Aquino, and pretty damn fast. She committed political suicide by involving the Americans. You're much more at risk from private score settling than from anything the government is likely to do. Keep your head down and watch your back, son. I'll make some calls. Let's see if we can find you a low profile posting for a couple of months. Last week no one would have taken my calls. Today it's a different story."

"Thanks, Tatay." Bongo was genuinely grateful. It was a rare thing for his father to acknowledge concern for his wellbeing. Most of the time, he just dealt criticism to his son for failing to measure up in one aspect of his life or another.

By 8 a.m., Captain Alejandro Mendoza and his men had formed ranks on Ayala Avenue, pointed in the direction of Fort Bonifacio, three miles away. On the stroke of the hour, he gave the order to march. As they wended their way, other groups of Rangers swelled their numbers, joining them from side streets.

Bongo was taken aback by the sight of civilians lining the sidewalk and applauding them. Someone started to sing the regimental fight song and the swelling column joined in. At a couple of key intersections, he noticed television crews covering the march. The thing was becoming a national spectacle. Even more extraordinary, they were two miles into the march when one of the government troops ostensibly policing the march broke ranks, ran over to him, and gave him a hug.

"This was a very brave thing you did, brother. I salute you."

Bongo, startled, returned the embrace stiffly. *If this is surrender, I'll take it any day of the week*, he thought, bewildered.

As they reached the fort, the column ground to a halt.

"What's going on?" Bongo asked. A soldier a few rows in front of him had turned around and was shouting something. He strained to understand what was being said. The message was relayed back by those able to hear.

"They're letting us into the fort a company at a time. Maybe they're worried if they let too many in at once we'll capture the place all over again," a cheerful youngster two rows ahead of him said. "You identify yourself, hand over your weapon, and you should be free to go. They're putting a few guys under arrest, but not too many it seems."

Bongo felt a ripple of anxiety. Would someone have reported him for gunning down those two soldiers?

Although it was just after nine, the sun was beating down on the stalled column. *It's going to be brutal out here in a couple of more hours,* Bongo thought. He cursed his lack of foresight at not bringing a canteen. *You'd think I would know better.*

As it turned out the lack of water was solved by the civilians and well-wishers who had gathered to watch the spectacle. Under the watchful eye of government troops, they were supplying drinks and snacks to the erstwhile rebels as they awaited processing. It was nearly noon before Bongo, having been relieved of his rifle and pistol, found himself in front of a desk in the open courtyard of the fort. He was questioned by a grizzled captain who made no effort to hide his disdain for the men appearing before him.

"Name and rank?" The officer, who was obviously a chain smoker, stubbed out his latest cigarette in an overflowing ashtray, before drawing a fresh one from a packet he kept in his vest pocket.

Bongo supplied the information. His interrogator consulted a typed list of names, running his finger down the page. Abruptly he stopped and stabbed at an entry. Then he looked up and regarded Bongo sharply. Without turning his head, he called out to one of the sentries who stood behind him. "Lieutenant Cruz is to be detained for further questioning. Escort him to the guardhouse."

Fuck, Bongo thought. *I should have gone on the run. They're going to nail me for those two clowns I gunned down.*

An escort marched him across the courtyard and locked him in one of the holding cells.

"How long am I going to be kept here?" he yelled as his captor turned to leave.

"You'll need to wait your turn, lieutenant," was all he got back.

It was after midnight when they came for him. Bongo had spent the intervening hours debating what he should and should not admit to. It was going to come down to those two idiots he had shot in the initial assault on the fort; he was sure of it. For a while, he considered denying being anywhere near the fort when it was seized, but he knew that would never hold up. There would be too many witnesses who had seen him. Even some of the guys ostensibly on his side would rat him out if they thought they would be treated more leniently. It was best to claim he was in a combat situation and two adversaries were approaching him armed and with lethal intent. It was kill or be killed.

He was dozing fitfully when someone roughly shook him by the shoulder and hustled him into a room empty but for a small table and two hard-backed chairs. An officer sat in one.

Bongo started to sit, rubbing his shoulders. The officer looked up sharply. "Remain standing, lieutenant. That's an order. And have you forgotten how to salute a senior officer?"

"No sir, sorry sir." Bongo came smartly to attention and saluted. The epaulettes on the man's shoulders indicated he was a full colonel, but Bongo didn't recognise him. His interrogator did not return the salute, busying himself instead by reading the file in front of him. Bongo was obliged to remain at attention for fully ten minutes before the officer addressed him again.

"At ease, soldier. You may take a seat."

Bongo did as he was told and eyed the colonel warily.

"You are 2nd Lieutenant Bartolomeo Cruz, 1st Scout Ranger Regiment?"

The tone of voice did not make it clear whether this was a statement or a question. Bongo played it safe and answered. "Yes, Colonel."

"You stand accused of participating in the recent insurrection against the elected government of the Philippines. In addition, you are specifically accused that on December 1st you killed two soldiers who were charged with the defence of this fort when rebel forces seized the premises."

"They were firing at me. I was only defending myself." Bongo was determined to keep his responses as short as possible.

"You admit to being present, then?"

"Yes," Bongo replied.

"We have eyewitness depositions which state that the two men you shot had not unslung their weapons and posed no threat as you claim. You killed them in cold blood." The look of malice and hatred in the officer's eyes was unmistakable now.

"That's not what happened. As I just told you, I was defending myself."

"So you say," his inquisitor was scornful. "You're going to take me through exactly what you claim happened, step by step. Start with how you arrived at the fort and go from there."

The interrogation went on hour after hour. The same questions were asked over and over again. The man in front of him was indefatigable. He chain-smoked as he posed his questions, rarely looking up from the folder on his desk. At some point Bongo needed to get up from the chair. He had lost the feeling in his legs, and he desperately wanted to take a piss. If he wanted to avoid the humiliation of wetting himself, he was going to have to grovel in front of this puffed-up bastard.

"Permission to use the latrine, sir?"

"You have a problem with your bladder or your bowels, lieutenant?" The question was accompanied by a sneer.

"No, sir." Bongo had to will himself to keep from squirming, such was the irresistible urge to relieve himself.

"Take him out before he shits himself," the colonel said dismissively to the two guards standing by the door.

When he returned, Bongo found that a new officer, a major this time, was waiting for him. "You want a cigarette?" he asked.

Bongo shook his head wearily. "I could use some water." He looked longingly at the pitcher on the desk. The major filled a glass and pushed it in front of him.

"We know you shot those men in cold blood, lieutenant. We can keep this up indefinitely and you will break eventually, so why not save everyone's time and just admit to what you did?"

Bongo made the same rote denials, and the questions continued. It was four in the morning before they finally took him back to his cell. They had interrogated him for sixteen hours straight.

As he lay huddled in a foetal position on the trestle bed, Bongo felt a wave of desperation flood over him. They were right, of course. It was a question of when, not if, they wore him down. That was if he lived that long. Members of the men's families would be only too willing to take their revenge while he lay there, essentially defenceless, if his guards were bribed.

They came for him again at eight the following morning. At eight the following morning, they came for him again. His original inquisitor sat at the desk, the fan above him moving the air ineffectually to cool the room as the humidity became oppressive, even that early in the day.

The colonel regarded him with distaste. "Straighten yourself up, lieutenant. You're a disgrace to your uniform."

I wonder how you'd look if you'd been interrogated for hours and then locked up in a cell with only a bucket to piss and shit in and no way to wash, you snot-nosed bastard.

"All charges against you have been dismissed. You are to report to Lieutenant General Tolentino, Eastern Mindanao Command,

Davao City. You are seconded to his personal staff for the next year."

It took a few moments for the significance of the order to sink in.

"How did...?" Bongo began to formulate a question, and then the penny dropped. His father, of course! The old man had pulled strings. The swiftly changing political winds had reinvigorated the Cruz family's influence and reach.

Thank you, Tatay.

"Your orders are being cut right now. There's a flight in two hours from Villamor Air Base. You are going to be on it. These two here—" The colonel jerked his head at the two armed guards behind him. "—will see that you are. Dismissed."

Bongo saluted smartly and turned on his heel. The colonel did not return the salute. He had already transferred his attention to the papers on his desk.

Chapter Twenty-Five

Josh looked around his apartment with a sense of relief. He had just been dropped off by taxi from the international airport. Coaches had evacuated them from the Peninsula Hotel under the terms of the truce. Most of the expats were choosing to stay in the terminal until they could arrange flights home. He was among the few returning to the city. The atmosphere of normalcy that surrounded the journey back to his neighbourhood was surreal. He had difficulty reconciling the sights and sounds of life going on around him with the bloody violence he had left behind just a few hours earlier.

The temptation to flee the country had been strong, but he forced himself to behave rationally. First of all, there was the matter of two thousand dollars in cash, his emergency fund, stashed in a jar in the kitchen, which he would never see again if he didn't retrieve it. Then he had no idea how his employer would react if he just showed up back in the States without permission. Lastly, there was Rita. The apartment was stark and lonely without her. Images of her making herself busy in the kitchen or lying curled up on the couch in the living room rose unbidden to his mind.

I've been really happy these past few weeks, he admitted to himself. *I can't leave things with her as they are right now. I just can't.* What to do? *First, I need a shower and some sleep. I'm dog-tired.*

Josh thought about phoning the office. *Fuck it. I'll check in later this afternoon. If I contact them now, they'll just want me to come in.*

He spent a long time in the shower. The flood of emotion he was feeling threatened to overwhelm him, and he found himself shaking, even though the water was scalding hot. The dominant sensation was that of relief, relief that he had survived the violence of the past 72 hours. This was coupled with a desire to flee this violent, alien country as soon as he could. A car backfired in the street as he towelled down and he instinctively shrank back to an inside wall, dropping the towel, the plasterboard cold against his naked back.

Get a fucking grip Josh, he admonished himself. He retrieved the towel, grabbed a beer from the fridge, and sat down on the couch. After a few deep breaths and a couple of swigs, his pulse stopped racing and his anxiety abated. As concern for his physical safety lessened it was replaced in his racing thoughts with guilt and shame for his fling with Roberta and total confusion about his feelings for Rita.

There had been a point in their relationship when he had seriously thought of making a long-term future with her. She made him feel happy, and wanted, and loved. It led him to minimise the differences in their backgrounds and race. *We're just two people after all,* he had thought to himself, but recent events had made it clear that he could not possibly live in the Philippines, which meant they would have to make their lives somewhere else. Josh had no more appetite for further foreign adventures. All he wanted was to return home and discard his passport. If he and Rita were going to have a life together, it would be back there. How would his parents react? He shuddered at the thought. His mother, the ultimate social climber, would be aghast.

"How could you throw yourself away on some Asian girl, a person of no consequence Joshua? You were raised with every advantage, and this is how I am to be rewarded?"

As for his father, Josh felt a cold rage rising in him. The sanctimonious prick would berate him for hooking up with a shiksa. The bastard had only got religious after the divorce. He now went to the synagogue every morning to make up the minyan for daily prayers. This excess of piety from a guy who could scarcely show up for services on Yom Kippur.

They had never hit it off. For a start, Josh had never been very interested in sports. His father had excelled as a wrestler, both in high school and later at Brandeis University. It didn't help that his brother Sam had taken to ice hockey and his father, though initially dubious, had fallen in love with the game, even going so far as to buy two season tickets for the Bruins. Josh had never been invited to accompany the old man. Ezra Steinberg was forever comparing Josh

A Coup in Manila

unfavourably with his two siblings and took every opportunity to run him down in front of friends and relations.

"Not the sharpest knife in the drawer is Joshua. I say it even if he is my own son. Absolutely no head for business."

Comments like that were the soundtrack of Josh's childhood. Ben would take his father's side whenever they disagreed. Only Ruth might offer sympathy for his perspective, and even then, it wasn't guaranteed.

As for how his friends would react to Rita, Josh winced as he thought about the snide comments he would be subjected to, along the lines of 'rent-a-girlfriend' or 'mail-order bride.' There was also bound to be a racist undercurrent in some circles. Did he really have the intestinal fortitude to face all this rejection?

Rita would be a fish out of water, totally dependent on him, if he uprooted her and moved her to the States. If he was honest with himself, he just wasn't ready for that sort of responsibility. He had great memories of the time they spent together, and he really felt a connection with her but in the end, it just wasn't going to be enough. Josh sighed. He would have to see her one last time. He owed her that much.

He briskly towelled off and collapsed naked into bed, not even bothering to draw the curtains. He was fast asleep as soon as his head hit the pillow.

A few hours later, the buzzer at his front door woke him up. He looked groggily around. It was dark outside and his watch showed it was just past 8 p.m. He blundered over to the intercom and pressed the button.

"Who is it?" he mumbled.

"It's me, Rita. I was worried about you. I heard on the radio they'd evacuated everyone from the hotel."

"Why didn't you just come on up? You have a key." Josh ran his hand through his hair, feeling anxious.

"The way we left things I thought I'd better knock."

"Come on up."

He raced back to the bedroom and ransacked a couple of drawers, desperately looking for a clean T-shirt. The only one he could find was a bilious shade of green but he put it on anyway. He slipped on his jeans and had just taken a swipe at brushing his teeth when he heard her come in.

Josh took a quick look at himself in the mirror. The face he saw was unshaven and looked tired. He grimaced and went into the living room to meet her. She looked beautiful. She was wearing a pale yellow, lightly floral-patterned dress and a small silver crucifix adorned her neck. They stood apart, regarding each other awkwardly. Then she stepped forward quickly and kissed him lightly on the cheek.

"I'm so glad you're safe."

Josh resisted the temptation to pull her firmly into an embrace. Instead, he kissed her lightly in return. Then he took her hands in his and drew her onto the sofa.

"I'm glad you came, Rita. We need to talk."

"Was the siege very frightening?" she asked.

"Not so much frightening as disorienting. I never thought I'd find myself in the middle of a war zone."

She nodded sympathetically. "I said some very harsh things when we last met. I'm sorry."

He sighed. "There was a fair amount of truth in it though, Rita. That's probably why it hurt so much."

"I've missed you terribly, Joshua. When I heard you were caught up in the siege, I was frightened something might happen to you." Rita looked at him, her eyes welling up with tears.

Josh rubbed his face and bit his lip. She frowned.

"Joshua, what's the matter?"

"The thing of it is, Rita…" he began lamely. Her eyes narrowed. She stiffened, withdrew her hands from his, and moved herself a little farther apart from him.

Josh spoke softly, almost mumbling. "I was having a hard time with the way of life in the Philippines before I got caught up in this whole coup business, but now…" He paused. "The setup here is so alien, so violent. I feel I just want to wrap some things up and get the hell out of here back to the States."

"And am I just one of the things you want to wrap up, Joshua?" Rita said, regarding him now coldly, an edge in her voice. He looked at her, agonised.

"Rita, I have feelings for you, the strongest feelings. You must know that. But we come from two totally different worlds. It's like the old Jewish saying, 'A bird may love a fish, but where would they live?' I can't imagine myself in your world, nor can I imagine you in mine."

"So, I was right all along," Rita said bitterly. "All I was to you was a paid companion. How could I have been so stupid as to let myself get emotionally involved with you? You know something, Joshua Steinberg? You're a coward. We could have had something together, you and I, but you don't want to leave your blinkered, comfortable world. In some ways, I pity you." He made as if to reply, but Rita was already on her feet.

"No. Don't say any more. They're just going to be more empty words. I'm sick of the platitudes, the empty promises. I never want to see you or hear from you again. The sooner you leave the Philippines the better." She spat the words out. Then she turned on her heel and left, banging the door behind her.

Josh was left alone on the couch, stunned and deflated at how the conversation had spun out of control. He stared dispiritedly at the door and felt a fresh wave of tiredness washing over him. Slowly, he got to his feet, wandered back into the bedroom and clambered fully clothed back into his bed, pulling the cover over his head and curling up like an embryo. Within a couple of minutes, he was asleep.

Josh woke reluctantly once more, this time to the ringing of the telephone. He thought about ignoring it, but the noise was incessant. The person calling showed no signs of giving up. He made for the kitchen, cracking his toe on a leg of the bed as he did so. The pain was agonising and he cursed volubly.

"Josh Steinberg speaking; who is this?" he asked sharply, hopping on one foot.

"Don't bite my head off, pal. It's Lou."

"What's up, Lou? Couldn't it wait until the morning?" Josh grumbled.

"I suppose it could, Josh, but I just thought you'd want to know we've been given our marching orders."

"What are you talking about, Lou?"

"Well, I, unlike some people I could mention, was at the office this afternoon. The data centre is being closed down, effective immediately. This coup fiasco was the last straw for the suits back at headquarters. They're sick of the Philippines. They've contracted for new premises in Mumbai."

"What did Webster have to say when I didn't show up?" Josh asked anxiously.

"He just assumed you'd already left the country. He can't wait to get his fat ass out of here himself. I volunteered to stay put and turn off the lights. I thought he was going to give me a blowjob he was so grateful."

"So, you're saying I can leave?" Josh said, a wild feeling of exultation overwhelming him.

"Soon as you like, ol' buddy."

"I'll contact the travel department back in the States. It's still early for them. With any luck I can leave tomorrow morning."

Lou whistled. "You are hot to trot, aren't you, Josh? Sorry to rain on your parade, old friend, but you may find flights back to the U.S. pretty booked up."

"I'll go the other way round if I have to," Josh said desperately. "To Europe somewhere, and across the Atlantic."

"Sounds a bit extreme for my tastes, Josh, but if you're really serious, I'd try Lufthansa. They fly every day to Frankfurt. Listen, call me back when you find out about flights. If you really are leaving tomorrow, let's make a night of it. We can get wasted, play some pool, and I'll pack you into a limo for the airport when we've closed the bar down. I've got some personal news I'd like to get off my chest before you take off."

Josh looked around his apartment and considered the suggestion. He had little to pack and could probably be done in an hour. Lou would be good company and he didn't feel like being on his own.

"Okay, Lou. But let's not go to Mogombo. I don't want to run into Rita. I'll let you know if I get lucky with flights."

"No worries, we'll hit up the Australian Embassy. They have a good pool table. Phone me as soon as you find out if it's a go."

It was after 9 p.m. when Josh finally swung open the door of the Australian Embassy. The renowned bar was in fine form. Games of strip poker, Jenga, darts, and pool were happening, and every girl in the place was engaged with a patron under the watchful eye of the mama-san.

Lou Holt was tucked away in a booth in the back of the room with two girls ostensibly hanging on his every word. He saw Josh enter and waved cheerily. Josh weaved his way between the tables, laden down by his suitcase and backpack.

"Grab a seat, Josh. This here is Suzie." Lou had an arm wrapped around a plump bar girl, who smiled slyly at the introduction. "I reserved Jasmine for you." He pointed with his head at Suzie's thinner companion, who visibly brightened at now having a punter of her own.

"Jasmine, stow Josh's gear behind the bar. Be sure to keep those bags safe now. He'll have a San Miguel to start with. Then, if you two girls can powder your noses for ten minutes, I just need a few words in private with my friend. After that, we're all yours." He leered suggestively. "The night is young, and who knows what mischief we can get up to?"

The girls got up as instructed and made themselves scarce.

"So, what's the big news, Lou?" Josh asked.

Lou was grinning from ear to ear. "Thing of it is, Josh, I asked Marta to marry me yesterday, and of course she said yes."

"You're not serious, Lou." Disbelief was written all over Josh's face.

"Sure am," Lou said pugnaciously, picking up on Josh's scepticism. "Oh, I know you think this place is a Godforsaken shithole, and you can't wait to get out of here, but I've been here longer than you, Josh. I've sort of fallen in love with the people and the way they look at life."

"But Marta is a hooker," Josh blurted out.

"What of it?" Lou shrugged. "I'm certainly no saint. Marta went into that line of work as one of the only ways she could make ends meet and be a support to her family. Initially we came to an arrangement that suited us both. She got some sort of stability and an income. I got sex on tap. Over time, though, we've started acting more like a married couple. I just decided to make it official is all. I like it here in Manila, Josh. With my skill set, I don't foresee any problem landing another job when this gig is done. I can see myself having a couple of kids with Marta and enjoying a very good lifestyle. Better probably than anything I could aspire to back in the States. When it comes right down to it, I'm a pretty traditional sort of guy."

"How can you say that, sitting in a glorified brothel with a couple of girls on tap, Lou?" Josh was genuinely confused.

"Them?" Lou glanced over at their two companions, who were waiting to be summoned. "A bit of harmless fun. The only woman I've been to bed with for the past six months is Marta."

"Well, if that's what you honestly feel, Lou, I'm very happy for you. I really am," Josh said, impulsively leaning over to hug his friend.

Lou beamed. "Thanks, pal. It means a lot. But enough about me. What's the story with you and Rita?"

"We're done. I'd just as soon not talk about it, Lou." Josh said, his eyes begging his friend not to press him.

Lou took the hint. "Fair enough. No more sentimental claptrap. Let's get this farewell party started."

It was 4:30 in the morning when Lou piled Josh, drunk and bleary-eyed, into a taxi for the airport. The journey, which had taken two hours when he first arrived—seemingly an eternity ago—took only twenty minutes, but even at that hour the departures hall was crammed. A couple of hours later, Josh took one last look at Manila as his plane gained altitude. Memories of his time with Rita came flooding back, and he was overwhelmed with feelings of loss and guilt. Tears welled up. He blinked and made as if to wipe a stray eyelash away to hide his embarrassment.

The place has changed me completely, he thought. *I don't know if it's been for the better. I wonder if I'll ever be back here again. Somehow, I doubt it.*

Chapter Twenty-Six

Rita listened wearily to her father's angry voice on the other end of the phone, straining to hear him over the raucous sounds of the bar in the background. She was back at Mogombo, having told her aunt and uncle that she had to return to her housemaid's job.

"The woman I work for is annoyed that I'm not there. She's threatening to fire me and get another girl in if I don't show up," she had said.

They had gone along with the polite fiction. She wondered if they believed it or not. Her aunt did, probably because she wanted to. Her uncle likely knew better, but was keeping his mouth shut. The necessity of resuming her role as a bar girl was only reinforced by what her father was saying.

"You need to be back at work, Rita. We need what you can send us more than ever. Eddie is gone. We can't mourn him forever. And now that the bastard who ran him over has got himself killed, that money he promised us is vanished. The fool was shot trying to flee the Peninsula Hotel. I talked to your bastard cousin Bongo about it. That arrogant prick as much as admitted to me that he was the one who fired the shot. The chance of all that money got thrown away

273

because the murdering bastard felt like administering his own brand of vigilante justice. A dead Englishman is not going to put food on the table. His money would have. We need you to be a dutiful daughter now, Rita. We really need the money you send us. Get extra work shifts if you can. Do you hear what I'm saying, Rita?"

"Yes, Tatay. I'll have some money to send you next week."

"Can you not do something sooner, Rita?" Her father's voice was plaintive.

"No, Tatay. I'm sorry. I just started back."

"I suppose it will have to do. Send as much as you can."

"I will, Tatay. I need to go now. My shift is starting." She put down the phone and began to cry.

Rita felt hopeless and desolate. Her future, bleak and sordid, stretched out in front of her. Her father's avarice was just a product of living in grinding poverty. He was a decent man in an impossible situation. She could not blame him.

Joshua had been a pipe dream. It was never going to work out. She had judged him harshly because she needed him to give her a chance at a better life, and he had been unable to surmount the obstacles between them.

This won't do, Rita, she told herself sternly. *You must pull yourself together and put your trust in God and his Holy Mother.*

She took a quick look in a mirror as she passed into the bar area. It was quiet with just a few patrons, all occupied with one of the other girls. After a few minutes, a youngish man, slightly chubby and sweating heavily, came in looking around uncertainly. He made his way to a stool at the counter and asked for a beer. The mama-san caught Rita's eye and gestured with her fan.

Rita came up beside him, and with a practised smile said, "Hello, my name is Rita. Would you like some company?"

Printed by Amazon Italia Logistica S.r.l.
Torrazza Piemonte (TO), Italy

60145217R00157